VINCENT BLACK

Dedicated to those who believed in me
when I didn't believe in myself.

TABLE OF CONTENTS

Each and every soul that has ever existed has a story. Some are fortunate enough to be shared through history, and those lucky enough are etched into legend. Documented by writers and scholars for generations.

Others are told not in books or classic tall tales. Stories of one's personal journey from birth to death. They are rarely shared at all, most kept to themselves by the author living it. These stories are still documented, though. Through conversations told on rough days, scribbles in forgotten journals, newspaper clippings, be them wedding announcements or obituaries, or even the occasional letter sent to an estranged friend or forgotten foe.

Everyone has a story to tell, and it is the job of those dedicated enough to collect the vital ones and compile them into an official record. To be used as an example of what one has done in this world, and as proof for their pending judgment.

Signs

PART ONE

THE DEVIL'S ORACLE

◆

The following letter was found in Benjamin Hornsworth's desk drawer in the spring of 1912.

DEAR FATHER,

The following tale took place last night. I think you might find it interesting. I was cleaning the confession booth when the silhouette of a middle-aged man entered the booth on the other side. He spoke with such frailty for a man of his age, almost as if I was speaking to a child.

"Forgive me, Father, for I have sinned."

The silence crept into the interior of the confession box. I could feel the wind die and the temperature become cold. I cannot explain why, but I was uneasy almost in an instant.

"I feel that my sin is too great for the Lord to forgive. I feel that I'm too wicked for the Lord to redeem. I strongly believe that when Jesus died for our sins, that he had to see and feel every sin committed and that it went by in all of a blur. I believe that Father. I believe that he saw every sin and even if it was just for a split second that he saw every sin ever committed. I know in my heart that is true. I also know that even though he saw everyone's sins for a split second, mine are so abundant and grotesque that he had to experience a whole minute of my crimes Father. I fear that he will never forget that."

I assured him that the Bible teaches us that once you repent that you are new. When God looks at you he does not see your past sin. He abolishes your sin, and he forgets it entirely. I told him, "Son, you are not in a battle with God. You need not feel like he hates you. He loves you. You are in a war with Lucifer, and you are foolish to let him win when all you need to do is forgive yourself as God has forgiven you." I remember how you toil with your grief and remember several conversations with you. I do not write this letter though to continue in my quest to help you see that. I write it for what happened next.

"Yes Father." He knew the answer, but just like you, couldn't accept it.

I asked him if he had asked for repentance. He let out full tears. "I have not father." I explained that the church was a forgiving one. That he was free to divulge what he wanted without fear of reports to the authorities. That we did not practice the "Catholic guilt" so abundant in the west and that we believe in redemption. His testament still haunts me.

"Father, I have been truly wicked." He paused, and inhaled a deep breath. "I have killed many men in my day."

I was going to ask if he fought in the war, but he didn't give me a chance to speak.

"I didn't fight in any war; I did it out of malicious intent. I have killed so many men." I asked him how many he had killed. "I couldn't even say. More than ten. I remember it started when I would hunt rabbits with my father. They would be out in the field, and at first, they were troublesome to catch. Then one day, the hunt was no longer fun. It was no longer enough. I first killed my brother. He was younger than me. He was my baby brother. I sent his body down the river with the knife still in him." He weeps. "My parents loved him more than me. He was five, and I was fifteen. I told my parents that he drowned swimming and that I tried to save him but that I failed. My parents didn't suspect a thing. Their grief denied the reality."

I told him that he would be forgiven. He cited that Cain was sent to hell after killing Abel, and that he had killed more than just his brother. That God banished Cain. I told him that he was correct, and that God did banish Cain. But I taught him about Jesus and his forgiveness, that man is redeemable when he accepts him in his life. I asked him if he was saved.

"As a baby," he replied.

I told him that it still counts. I then asked him what I always ask those who were raised in the faith. "Do you believe that Jesus is your savior?"

"I did, father."

I asked him what had changed. His next course of action still haunts me now. My hand trembles as I try to document it. His posture changed. He no longer seemed fragile or vulnerable. The silhouette became darker, and his shoulders appeared broader as his head grew thinner. His voice grew deeper, and a man of evil began to speak.

"There was a man who lived down the road from my family. A wretched man. He would come around to all of our houses and try to sell his putrid "goods". The man was despicable, a fraudster and a fool! He overpriced his cheese and was rude to the children. The women all loved him though, including my Elizabeth. I had heard rumors at the pub that he was sleeping around with people's wives when they were out laboring during the day. I didn't think I would have to worry about my wife because she was faithful. I never thought to think about my sweet daughter Elizabeth, for she was too young. She was twelve, a child. Thomas McHugh was the devil himself. It was only proven to me when I found my Elizabeth near death in the alley behind his house. She was beaten to a pulp, naked in the street. Her wonderful singing voice left to a faint moan that reeked of pain. It was then when I decided that I was going to kill this devil once and for all."

The man continued to tell his story, but I swear, that as I can recall, the silhouette of the man had disappeared into the darkness as his voice still bellowed out. The whole ordeal was surreal to me, like I was living a dream.

"I stayed up late waiting for him to return to his home. He entered the door drunk, he was stumbling around like the fool he was. He found his way to a chair near the fireplace. It was a cold night, but my body became adjusted to the frigid shadows in my wait. He went to strike a match to start a fire. As he tossed it into his fireplace, the oil I had put in the fire erupted like a door being opened in a dark room. Instantly, there was light everywhere. The fire spread to the walls, drapes, and ceiling. I didn't want the devil to think that I had defeated him on earth; I wanted to show him that in the domain of Hell, I was still his nightmare. He turned around, and as I raised my ax into the air. I let it hang there, and he stared at it like he was staring at the stars, amazed at its wonder. I brought it down on his leg so hard that it got stuck in the floor. He howled like a rabid dog. I chuckled with the joy of a child. I removed my ax and began to swing violently at his chest. Trying to make as much of a mess, to cause as much pain as I could. I drove the ax blade straight up his cock and turned it like I was cranking down on a valve. I continued to swing with relentless fury. I cut off each limb with anger that can only come from a caged man. By the time I lifted my ax to cut off his head, I realized that he had been dead for several minutes. His face was frozen in a place of pure terror. I had seen that same face before. It was the look on my brother's face when I was stabbing him with my mother's kitchen knife. The pure shock and pure morbid fright that haunts my eyes to these days. As I stared at my brother's face in the burning inferno, I realized that I had not come to kill the devil; I had become him."

I remained silent and wiped the sweat off my brow.

"You see, Father, I do not believe that Jesus is my savior. Jesus despises the work of the devil. Jesus came to save man; he did not come to save monsters. He may be your savior, Father, or of my daughter, but he did not come to save me. He came to save the world from men like me."

The silence crashed down in the booth like an ocean suffocating me. I tried to conceive a thought, but my mind was in a state of survival. It had been years since I had seen such an evil up close. Before I could impart counsel to the man, he exited the booth. When I opened my door to try to chase after him, he was gone. The church was empty, and all the candles were out. The star light shining through the windows was all I could use to see.

I write you this letter today, father, not in hopes of scaring you. I know you are not easily frightened by the tricks of Lucifer. But I write it to warn you that I believe Lucifer knows that you will soon be visiting our church and our town. I believe that he is scared, and in his cowardice, he has tried to scare me and as a result, try to warn you from coming here. It only makes me wish that you come sooner than you intend. However, I do fear that perhaps in some way that it is a trick for him to get a hold of you again.

Sincerely, Father Valentine.

An Undelivered Letter

The following letter was found in the Valentine Estate in the winter of 1930. Helen is often referred to in Greek Mythology as the most beautiful woman to have ever lived.

Dear Helen,

To say that I have missed you is an understatement. It has been a while since our last visit. My work has been keeping me from the city you call home. Work has been demanding, and we have seen little reward. The people we do save usually stay quiet and many fear so heavily that they believe that God is not enough.

I am afraid that Leopold is growing more desperate with his attempts, showing the same reckless behavior of our youth. His actions get more messy and grandiose. It is not the tactical, small-scale operations as once before. I fear that he will one day learn of your location.

My sweet Helen, I do not know what I would do with myself if I were to lose you. I fear that you are the only thing that keeps me sane and collected in this world and that if I ever lost you, I would be just as much a monster as Leopold. Helen, you are as beautiful as the sunrises that I miss sharing with you.

With much love, your grateful fool.

The John George Letter

———————◆———————

*This letter was compiled in a binder entitled
"Proof of an Afterlife" on the Valentine property.*

Dear Father Valentine,

Please forgive me for contacting you on behalf of your father, the count. We have been very busy these last few days. The mess in the hillsides is much larger than we feared. Your father has been very quiet. If I didn't know him personally, I would fear that he was just as terrified as the people we have come across.

The people are spreading rumors about a beast that strikes down sinners and innocent alike. Many oppose your father in fear of him being the beast. It would help if he could speak to them during the day. I tell your father that the rumors spread about him are far worse than the truth. Still, he disagrees. Through some convincing, some will come to his midnight sermons. Your father will never admit it, but I can tell that he wishes you had joined us on our voyage. Father Abe has had trouble connecting with everyone, including your father.

The story you shared with your father is quite puzzling to me. As a young boy, I recall hearing a similar tale. My brother would talk about Thomas McHugh's grizzly murder. My brother was amazed by the testimony given by John George, the man who admitted to the murder. It was passionate and genuine. The man had taken pure joy in telling what he had done to Thomas. My brother called it a performance on the stand. Two elderly men on the jury passed away during the trial. Many thought that the confession scared them to death, while others believed that they didn't wish to live any longer in a world where such evil exists.

As I read your tale, I shivered as I feared that if you were speaking to John, then the devil's role in this evil would be more prevalent than I had assumed. John George was sentenced to death two decades ago. My brother watched him hang and told me the judge wanted him cremated. Therefore, there would be no body for the afterlife. It was these events that caused my brother to come to the faith. He told me, "If John George isn't the devil, then let every man know that the devil's wickedness is more than any poet can imagine, and that man's only hope is in the teachings of Christ." My brother's new found faith did not just inspire those he had shared it with in his remaining years. But he also rekindled my faith during a dark period of my own.

I fear the devil may haunt us with our own personal John George's. He must truly be afraid of your father and our revival to go to such extremes.

With Best Regards, Benjamin Hornsworth.

Father Abe's Letter Concerning Mislav

A former priest by the name of Douglas O'Carroll died with this letter in his pocket. The first black man to be buried in a Church graveyard in the United States.

This letter is addressed to Count Valentine, let those who read it never have to suffer to the extent of its understanding.

When Mister Hornsworth first contacted me for this mission, I happily accepted. Not for the small fortune you promised my parish but for the chance to bring the Lord's word to ears that never heard it. I know we haven't seen eye to eye in the matter of our presence here. I have asked for permission to leave several times but have always been reassured that God's words would be planted and that he is on our side. I write this letter in hopes that you will reconsider my request for leave from this village. That this tale will show my impatience is not getting the better of me. That something far worse has.

The great fire that struck these mountains has destroyed these peoples' faith. When I arrived here, I thought we were helping these poor villagers recover, that we would show God's grace. I preach every day to men and women who have fear in their eyes. They only give me stares of surrender. Their hands still tremble after weeks. I have heard you give sermons in the night that have strengthened my convictions. Arguments of faith crafted so beautifully they could make the most brutal men from my town surrender to the Lord. Yet the people here still walk the streets with defeat. I know I have mentioned these concerns before, but I feel I need to repeat them in this plea for a return home. If this is not alone enough reason I have to include the tragedy of Mislav.

Mislav was a local farmer. He came to me the other day asking for him, his wife, and three children to be baptized. His eyes had the same fear in them as so many others. I told them that I could baptize them and that it would be an honor. I spent the day at his farm teaching them more about the faith, and before sunset, I baptized him and his family in a little creek on his farm. Mislav told me that I had to come over for dinner the following day. That he would bring out his best wine and meat for the occasion. I told him that it was not necessary, but he insisted.

I returned to our quarters that night, believing that this mission was worth it. Maybe the seeds of our faith can be planted here. The next day I returned to his farm, the sun was coming down, and I noticed a small campfire in one of Mislav's fields. I walked towards it, and when I came across the fire, I noticed a single man standing behind it. He was smoking a cigar and wore old tattered black clothes.

"Are you a friend of Mislavs," I ask?

The man replies, "I am no friend to anyone." I ask his name and what he is doing on Mislav's farm. The man starts to walk away towards the creek. I follow after him to see what he does. He leads me to the creek where I baptized the family the day before. There is another fire near the shore. As we get closer, I can smell a rancid smell. The fire continues to grow as we approach.

This stranger walks slowly but not with the same defeat as the people we've been seeing. He walked with ease and confidence.

We came around the bend, and on the creek bed where I had baptized him, Mislav kneeled next to his child's corpse with a knife. He continued to plunge it over and over again in the girl's chest. He was crying. I stood shocked in place, I fear to admit, doing nothing. He grabbed his daughter and threw her on the fire. I then noticed that his wife and youngest daughter were already lying dead in its flames.

His only son sat silently next to the fire. Mislav grabbed him by the shoulder and carried him to where he once was before. The son laid down with no care. Mislav reached for his knife, and I broke from my shaken state and screamed to stop. He does not hear me. I screamed at him not to do it as I began to run towards him. I cried and argued with him, but it led me to nowhere but madness, for Mislav does not even acknowledge my presence.

Mislav holds the knife up in the air as I reach him. I grab him and tell him to stop. He stabs me in my shoulder. I fall back to the ground. The pain made it hard for me to speak, yet I still begged. "Mislav, there's no reason to do this!" I scream. Why? I yelled at him and God. Mislav slams the knife down into his son. His son gives out a scream. His father lunges down his knife with a blast of fear, and then another and another. I try to stop him, but I fall unconscious from my wound.

I woke up later to find the fire still burning. The mysterious man continued smoking his cigar. My cut has healed as if it never happened. I see Mislav crying in a pool of blood. I asked the man what had happened. The man took his time to speak, first looking at me, then at Mislav.

"I gave him something you could not. I assure you there is nothing you can do now to save him."

Mislav began to scream with the anger of a beast. He got up on his feet and walked towards the fire. I screamed at him. "Mislav, you have no need to do this! God can still forgive you! I can help you! Allow him a chance!" Mislav didn't bat an eye or miss a step. He continued to walk and spoke to me with the eyes of the damnation of the flame.

"Father, God does not save monsters."

He walked into the fire, and night surrounded me. I had never prayed like I did that night. I screamed in agony in that field to God. Praying for Mislav and his family to be forgiven. I begged him for an answer as to why this was happening. I had never felt such rage and dread in my entire life. God was silent as he usually is. I sat in my tears and sweat and thoughts.

I knew at this point that I could not stay here. I asked around the next day, and no one could tell me of Mislav and his farm. I was stuck with the idea that I may have had a bad dream or that evil forces were trying to force me to leave. Deacon Christanson told me that this black figure had appeared to him once in a dream. I still have doubts that it was a dream. All I know is that whatever was sending this message to leave, I think they have won. My work here, my message is never going to be planted. The seeds that perhaps prove prosperous will be stomped on by evil before they can become saplings. I have failed you, myself, the Lord Almighty and I have failed Mislav. Please reconsider my request for release.

Father Abraham.

The Hole in My Hand

The following poem was nailed to the door of the Count Valentine Estate on a cold dark night.

I have carved a hole in my hand.
Not as deep as I wish, nor as wide as intended.
There is a line in my palm where this hole sits.
A line that rings with pain when my hand is
bended.
A punishment too small for the crime it fits.
See, I have done such horrible things,
Things worthy of crucifixion.
An act most known for its deliverance, and
not as an ancient, cruel punishment.
I could never be crucified now,
I can barely make a hole in my hand,
so I let others suffer.

Father Reynolds
Goodbye to Home

◆

Buried with Mary Reynolds.

Dear loving mother and father,

I write you this letter hastily with great news. Today a wealthy man by the name of Hornsworth came into town. He was searching for young preachers who would go on a mission in the mountains. Those who could speak gospel. My prayers have been answered. He promises riches to our parishes or our families. Soon you shall receive the first of many payments.

I don't have much time before I have to leave, so I apologize for my frantic writing. I am not sure how long it will take and when I will return home to see you. Tell Mathias and Rosaline that I will continue to pray for them, remind Rosaline to take care of my soon to be nephew and remind my brother that an extra mouth to feed is a blessing and not a worry.

Mother, please take care of father and continue to spread your overflowing joy. Father, please know that I journey now not in rebellion but in the rehabilitation of my wicked deeds. The Lord has forgiven me and given me a fresh start. I do not wish to destroy this opportunity. I hope that this new opportunity will help me prove to you the seriousness of my words. I pray that this journey brings much needed guidance to myself and an ease of worry to my family.

Love your son, Jeremiah Reynolds

The Decline of Bishop Gregory of Burryfield

*The following letter was in the wreckage
of a burned church in Burryfield.*

To whom it may concern;

I have received writings from Mr. Hornsworth,
Father Valentine, and other members of your
missionary party in regard to holding a service
at our Cathedral in the coming month. At this
point, I must decline your requests to do so.

From what I have gathered from my Church
members and local politicians, the organization
you represent is ill-organized enough to be a
proper one. As well as your claim to a ministry, as
established by several eyewitness testimony that
state such oddities as preaching in the middle
of the night. Our local doctors state that people
who have been "cured" by so-called "miracles"

often seem to get dangerously ill. Our town and cathedral's population want no business or association with whatever tonic you're peddling.

An official statement has been dispatched to our Church members and organizations through this great land. The statement reads as follows:

GREETING MEMBERS,

THE INSTITUTION OF OUR FAITH AND RELIGION IS UNDER ATTACK BY IMPOSTERS OF THE CROSS. THE COUNT VALENTINE REVIVAL AND THEIR MISSIONARIES DO NOT SPEAK FOR OUR CHURCH, OUR RELIGION OR OUR GOD. THEY SPEAK OF BLASPHEMY AND ONLY EXIST TO DECEIVE AND STEAL YOUR HARD EARNED MONEY.

THE CHURCH ISSUES THIS WARNING TO HELP IN SAVING YOU FROM TOTAL DAMNATION AND FROM THE CUNNING TRICKS OF THE DEVIL HIMSELF.

WE ISSUE A WARNING TO ALL CHURCH MEMBERS AND MEN OF THE CLOTH TO NOT ASSOCIATE WITH THIS PARTY. ANY ACCOUNTS OF ACTIVITIES WITH THIS PARTY WILL RESULT IN THE REMOVAL OF YOU FROM THE ORGANIZATION OF OUR CHURCH.

IF YOU NOTICE ANY SUSPICIOUS ACTIVITY FROM THIS PARTY, PLEASE ALERT THE AUTHORITIES AND LOCAL CHURCH. YOUR HELP IS NECESSARY IN RIDDING OUR COMMUNITY OF SUCH EVIL.

WE KEEP THIS IN OUR PRAYERS THAT GOD HELPS US IN SEEKING TRUTH AND REFUGE FROM SUCH EVIL.

Hopefully, this provided literature can help you understand the position of the church more clearly. We hope you will reconsider visiting Burryfield and its surrounding areas.

Finally, a word for Count Valentine himself. I understand that you find yourself to be a man of great faith, although strictly going by actions, I find you anything but.

Does a man of faith hide in the shadows and only preach occasionally in the dead of night? Does a man of great faith steal from the poor due to his own greed? Does a man of faith hide from his doubters and only allow communication through his subordinates? Does a man of faith poison fellow Christians in the hopes of selling dirty water for riches?

Are these the actions of our Lord and savior? Which a man of great faith would try to emulate to the best of his abilities.

You have been quoted as being a member of our church at one point and that you once held the title of a priest in the walls of a church in Italy. I have contacted holy men from various towns of the stated country and have only heard responses that prove the opposite. No such church records exist that prove your claims, and all members with your surname have been accounted for.

I do not know what devious plans you have for our city and the surrounding area, but know that you have made a very powerful enemy. Not only in our Church, but in the eyes of God as well.

Bishop Gregory of Burryfield

The Inglorious Bastards

PART TWO

THE ONE WHO
LIVES ABOVE

◆

A short story found in a collection in the Sundry Library. The fictional piece was written by Bishop Gregories sister, Julia Gregory sometime after she left the Church.

It's cold outside, and I hear thunder rolling in the distance.

This is supposed to be a privilege, a gift. That's what I keep telling myself. It's my seventeenth birthday, and I have been chosen to receive the mask from the one who lives above. My father's voice speaks of pride, but his face shows sadness. My mother holds me hourly with a love that tells me she doesn't want to let go.

Our town has several superstitions. We don't burn wood; we believe it releases the evil spirits of the trees. We don't blow out candles; we believe that each candle we light is a life and that we have no authority to end life. We knock on doors only two times, and we believe those with cruel intentions knock in threes. We don't waste water; they believe each drop is the tear of the one who lives above.

The one who lives above in the small shelter at the summit of our mountain has become too old to carry on. She rang the bell from the top of the mountain exactly ten days ago. Tradition states that when the one who lives above rings her bell, the oldest unmarried girl in the town must journey up the mountain to take her place.

I was going to be married once. He had my father's blessing. He had the most attractive eyes. The eyes of a dreamer. Unfortunately, he died in the war before he could ever ask me to complete his. A tragedy.

My father packs me a sack of everything I'm allowed. He hugs me for the last time. He whispers in my ear, "I know you will be alright". He turns around, and for a second, I see tears on my father's face for the first time. When he turns around, they are gone, and his eyes can no longer look into mine.

My mother gives me a loaf of bread, wrapped in our finest blanket. A good luck charm and the traditional gift for the one who lives above. "You are making our family proud; I wish I could be in your shoes". My mother speaks with pride, but her voice cries of loss. I look into her eyes for the last time, sketching them into my brain forever. My father grabs me and begins to comfort her as I say my final goodbye and walk away from my home.

As I walk out of town onto the mountain trail, I am greeted by flower petals on the path. My neighbors lay them before me as a gesture of goodwill, hoping that the sight of flowers on the mountain would remind me of their generosity. That I will continue to cry so that they are allowed to have rain for good harvests.

I was told it would be a long walk, but my dread, anxieties and constant fear made the time fly by. Before I could come to terms with the idea of living in solitude, the shelter was in front of me. The big bell hoisted over the shelter.

The bell rings two times. This means the one who lives above me sees me, and serves as a sign to my family that I had made it safely to the shelter. I make my way to the front door and knock two times. The door slowly opens. She is the oldest woman I have ever seen. Her gray hair flows from underneath her mask.

The one who lives above wears a mask covered in tears. It is attached to a crown that rests on top of her head. A single unit made out of wood and gems that resemble teardrops. Something that once was only a myth was now a fact of life staring me back in the face.

I handed over the bread my mother had prepared, and before a single greeting had been exchanged, the one who lives above fell to the floor with the bread. Devouring it like a hungry mouse eats the cheese next to his fallen friend. I've seen wolves devour chickens with more generosity.

I looked around the shelter as the one above all continued to feast. I notice a fireplace in the corner, it's not burning rags like at home, but wood. I notice half-burnt candles placed around the room. I see a cup of water slowly spilling out on a nearby table. The traditions of my family and people are not observed in the shelter.

"Do you not believe in evil spirits?" I question the one who lives above.

Her voice is frail and slow. She speaks like her will has been broken. "I do not believe in anything anymore. I have never been visited by an evil spirit when I burn wood. Even when I taunt and dare them to do their worst. I've blown out a candle every day since I was first sent to this shelter in hopes that it would end my life early, but alas, I am the oldest creature to ever reside in this shelter. I've cried into this mask for days during the summer but have never been able to make it rain, but when I'm happiest in the springtime, it rains. Everything I was ever told was a lie, I have stayed up here for as long as I can remember. We are just a symbol their faith and serve as a warning to the girls of that town to not go unmarried. No, I do not believe in your evil spirits; I believe man is the only evil spirit."

She gets off the floor and sits on a chair looking out on the town and nature below. "You have no idea at all. What I have had to give up, but you will. I am so sorry." She takes the mask off her face and extends it out to me. Her eyes are that of a younger woman begging for help. "It is your turn to wear this burden."

"Why? If none of it is true, then why do we continue this? Why do I have to lose my future?" I beg. She begins to close her eyes. She is so very tired. "Because if we do not, they will be lost." I put on the crown.

None of this is what I expected today. I expected to learn some great knowledge, to experience some ancient traditions. That I would be able to meet the one who lives above, the one who could make it rain with her tears and yet I just met another scared woman who misses her family.

I sat for a few minutes looking out the window. I see my old home. I know that I will never be able to return. That I will never be greeted with my father's smile again, and that I will never feel the safety of my mother's hug. I begin to cry.

It's cold outside and I hear thunder rolling in the distance. It begins to rain.

A Grave Letter

◆

Found in the pocket of Victor Peterson, hanged two months after its writing.

DEAR FATHER,

I am writing today with urgent information. As I am sure you will soon be notified, the Church leaders in Burryfield are displeased with your cause and have scorned you in the public's eyes. My association with you has led them to strip my title of priesthood. Do not worry though, for a member of my church is providing for me until I can reconnect with you.

This letter is sent to you urgently due to the news that broke out late last night. I was alarmed by shrieks from the city streets, and when I made my way outside, I could feel the smoke in my eyes. In the distance, the Cathedral of Saint Burryfield was burning. I am sad to inform you that it was not a small fire, and due to our limited use of firemen due to most being gone up north with forest fires, it only grew and grew until the point of oblivion.

I sat on the hill nearby, watching, crying and praying with the town's people. The fire had grown to the point of no return. The firemen began focusing on preventing the spread of the fire to surrounding buildings. It was a tragedy, and as of now, still no one knows how it started for sure.

My gracious Church member Victor woke me up this morning with grave news. Bishop Gregory had issued a statement accusing your ministry as the culprit of the crime. The lawmen of Burryfield have issued a reward for information about the fire and are actively searching for anyone associated with you. Victor has agreed to hide me until tonight when I can escape to the woods towards Heethburg for safe refuge.

Father I know you are not one to rush to anger or violence, but the stories you shared with me of your past lets me know that the temptation must still be there. I pray that you are not rushed with your response and that you take time to think of a proper response.

Sincerely, your son

An Inglorious Bastard Sets Cathedral on Fire

A newspaper article by the Burryfield Chronicle, the morning after the destruction of the Burryfield Cathedral.

The City of Burryfield is in distress this morning after the destruction of a temple of God was burnt down by an inglorious bastard. The Cathedral of Saint Burryfield was reportedly first seen set ablaze at dusk last night and burned until early morning.

The Burryfield police force has not released any official information about how the fire began, and the lead inspector has declined to make a comment. The inspector has put out a reward for any revealing information regarding the fire and has an official search for any members of the Valentine Revival Ministry.

Bishop Gregory, the leader of the local Church and caretaker for the Cathedral, commented to the press that he is "heartbroken and disgusted by the cruel act." The Church is raising money for the construction of a new cathedral.

The Church issued a warning to its members two days prior about the Valentine Revival Ministry. Stating that they "only exist to deceive" and are a threat to their religion. The Bishop of Burryfield has stated to his Church and the public that he believes the fire to be set by a member of the Valentine Revival, "perhaps even the Count himself."

Witnesses do attest to the fact that they saw a hooded man hurling rocks wrapped with flaming rags through the cathedral stein windows around dusk last night. However, neither the local fire department nor law enforcement have confirmed the cause of the fire or any description of the man seen by some witnesses.

The Burryfield Chronicle could not reach the Valentine Revival Ministry for comment by the time of publication. The ministry is a traveling one, believed to be in the hills north of the area. Providing aid to the small farming villages struck by the forest fires.

Count Valentine's only son, Johnathan Valentine, was a former priest for the church at a local parish in the eastern part of Burryfield. According to Bishop Gregory, he was expelled from the church because his relationship with his father raised "too many questions about his commitment to the church and its members."

"We do not know how many Johnathan Valentine has seduced into his father's cult, we must suspect anyone who is close to him and treat them as much of a threat as him and his father," Bishop Gregory continued to reassure the church's members. "We must not let ourselves live in fear, or the enemy wins. We must have no fears, for we know that the heavenly Father is watching over us and provides protection. As tragic as this destruction is, a Church is more than a building, it's a people and a community. We will not let this stop the mission God asks of us."

The Church is accepting donations at its east and southern parishes for the reconstruction of the cathedral. Extra services will be added to each parish to accommodate the increase in visitors.

THOMAS EDWIN
1804-1843

◆

*Obituary clipping found in the office
of Judge Paul Mathis.*

Thomas Ray Edwin, 39, was pronounced dead on February 23rd, 1843, at the Burryfield gallows. Thomas was born in Heethburg on January 2nd, 1804, to Eleanor and Glen Edwin.

He was raised in Heethburg and grew up on his father's farm outside of town. He enjoyed the outdoors and was an active member in the local Church. Thomas ran a small lumber business in the town of Burryfield for the last fifteen years.

Thomas moved to Burryfield at a young age and quickly established himself as a presence at the local cathedral. Helping in gathering donations and establishing a youth choir. He was married to his wife, Carolyn, at the cathedral in 1822.

Thomas is survived by his wife Carolyn, his father Glen, and his uncle Michael. He is preceded in death by his mother Eleanor, and his son Nathaniel.

His wife states that he will be missed forever and believes he is in heaven with their son.

A Proper Response

A copy of a letter sent to Bishop Gregory by Count Valentine, a copy of the letter was saved in Mr. Hornsworth desk, the original copy was burned by the Bishop in secret. He claims to never have received it.

Kind Greetings, Bishop Gregory,

There must have been a miscommunication or falsehood that you have received about my character, for I am afraid of no enemy. As a man of great faith, I believe that I am on the side of the Lord Almighty and therefore have no reason to fear or worry about your Church's prosecution.

Firstly I must express my deepest condolences to the Church and the people of Burryfield. The cathedral there was one of exceptional beauty and has brought many to the Lord. I still remember watching it be built, an incredible work of labor and innovation. Although I do suppose you will not believe that, or my following remark. To my knowledge and investigation, I wish it to be known that no one in my ministry committed such an act. We disdain violence and arson, and I promise you if it were to come forward that one of our members was involved, we would release them to the authorities immediately.

Secondly, it is odd that none of your holy men in Italy has a record of me, but not surprising. For I was a priest in the small town of Stabiea, but unfortunately, some years after I left the church, the town was lost to natural causes. Possibly destroying any affiliation, I would have had with the Church. I know you have no faith in me and no reason to, for I am a stranger. I promise you, Bishop Gregory, that I have made a similar oath to the savior and plan to live my life in accordance with his ways. I pray that both of our ministries are blessed with growth and continue to share the good word.

Thirdly I do understand that you find some of my ministries practices odd. Maybe more myself than my ministry. My ministry and I are not as peculiar as you might think. I would like to correct some of the misinformation you have heard. For one, we do not give any tonic to the people we preach to unless you count red wine for communion a tonic. We also do not charge any of the people we help for our services, or take any tithing. For we believe that we are here to do the Lord's work, and it is not right of us to charge since the lord is providing us with our payment of eternal life.

I was once a rich man, and although I still have a fortune in the eyes of a few, I do not use it selfishly or hold it like a miser. I give it to the priests to pay them for their time away from their families and to let them help their own communities and parishes. I also pay for their boarding and the food provided to them, as well as the food and supplies provided to the families we seek to help. I could go and describe all my charitable giving, but I am a humble man, and I only state what is above in hopes of proving the validity of my organization.

Now I know you have reservations about my nighttime preaching. Although it may seem odd, I do find it effective. For one the cold air allows for a calm setting and a place so devoid of light is the one that so much needs it. The work of the Lord is not confined to the daylight. Troubled souls are less likely to put on a mask during the night. Troubled souls are more likely to ponder during the night on their actions, for it is easier to reflect than to act. Those intimidated by the gazes of others and their own guilt find comfort in it. I hope this explanation suffices and puts some of your worries about me and my organization to ease.

Lastly, I must acknowledge the statement published by the Church and endorsed by yourself. I fear that the Church may have acted too rashly in its publication. Although rumors and stories may sound threatening to your organization, I must remind you that they are just stories. Hopefully, you and your fellow bishops can reflect on the statement and my words. In good time I do hope that our organizations can be stronger because of each other.

Attached to my letter is a generous donation to the rebuilding of the cathedral. I hope that I will once again be able to see it again in my lifetime. I also hope that in a month, once my travel brings us to Burryfield, the Church will welcome us. We still continue to request the use of a parish of yours for a mass, with financial compensation, of course. Although with your new situation, we will understand if they are too busy to undergo an extra service. If not, there is a theater owner or two who may be able to help us out in terms of a church, and if not, a fellow Christian who has land big enough for an outdoor service, for the Lord will always provide. Thank you for your reconsideration, and my ministry will be praying for your affected community.

Sincerely a Man with Great Faith

The Strigoi

A tale considered folklore in Eastern Europe,
the following rendition was told by Bram O'Carroll.
Exactly one year before his death.

No one knows for sure what a strigoi's true form looks like. No one knows when they will attack. No one knows why they do what they do. No one knows why they are so vicious to their victims. One thing is for certain, though; you don't want to be caught in their path.

These creatures are said to have not been created by God, but by the great evil himself. Created to pray on man's hate and fears. They cause havoc and fire to feed off your fear, like a cat playing with a scared mouse.

They look like you or I, and some even claim that they were once men themselves. No one can be sure who they can trust. That's why my grandfather always told me not to talk to strangers at night.

My grandfather narrowly survived an encounter with one of these creatures. He was a child when it happened. Traveling with his family to a new town in a stagecoach. It was dark, and there was thunder keeping him from sleeping.

In one instance, a peaceful night turned into carnage. At first, all my grandfather could hear was the scream of the horses. The coach started to increase in speed and shake as the horses desperately tried to escape from their reigns. His mother awakened from her sleep and started to scream, like waking from a bad dream. Unfortunately for her, the nightmare was just beginning.

All of sudden, the scream stopped. The vehicle became motionless, and darkness crept in. The lanterns no longer revealed his surrounding areas. My grandfather told me he could not see a foot in front of him and that it was like being blinded, not sure of the threats that could be lurking around. He called out to his mother.

It was quiet, and he made his way to the window by touch alone. He could feel the cold glass on his fingers, but couldn't see anything. It was as if he had been transported to a black void.

The silence and darkness startled him to his core. Again he called out to his mother.

Nothing happened. The darkness seemed to creep closer towards him. It transforming from a void to a living creature. He called out to his father this time.

The silence was deafening. Leaving him in a state of panic. My grandfather would tell me that he had felt like he had died at that moment, and that he was stuck in some sort of purgatory or hell.

The darkness was slowly illuminated by an amber glow. From the window, he could see the beginnings of a forest. A sigh of relief washed over him, as he felt that he wasn't taken from the world. The glow grew brighter and illuminated more and more.

My grandfather looked across the coach to find his mother's body lying motionless. Her neck was outside of the window with her shoulders pinched between the frames of broken glass. Her hands were frozen in space, each finger curled and broken to the back of her hand. Her head was dangling from her neck, just outside of view. A web of skin and tendons holding it there.

The amber glow grew and grew. My grandfather soon realized that the stagecoach was on fire. The heat was slowly rising, and it became harder to breathe. He was terrified. Not sure if he wanted to stay and die in the flames, or take his chance on whatever beast had slain his mother. His hope was whatever creature did, this would be gone by now. So he kicked through the door and started to run towards the forest. Behind him, he heard the cry of his father.

He turned around and saw his father on top of the stagecoach. His throat clenched in the hand of a silhouetted man. This creature's body retained no light and was taller than any man my grandfather had seen. The creature's other hand was tearing apart the chest of my great-grandfather. His blood dripped down the creature's claws. This beast appeared to be drinking the blood with the same glee as a drunk.

My grandfather was horrified at the sight of his father's death. His terror could no longer be confined. A scream beckoned from his heart.

The creature turned his head at my grandfather. Revealing prongs on top of his head, like those of a deer. My grandfather ran into the woods behind him and didn't dare to stop sprinting. He said it was like a wave of darkness was chasing after him. The branches of the trees swooped down to grab him, and the ground felt like it was sinking beneath him. Eventually, the whole forest collapsed in on him.

He was found a few days later by a hunter. Brought to the nearest town. He spent his days in an orphanage, where he eventually met his wife. A husk of a man. He didn't speak much when I knew him, and when he did, he would ramble about the terrors he saw. Many were convinced that he was mad. Creating a story to cope with his parents abandoning him. My father would assure me that strigoi weren't real and that his dad was losing his grasp of reality. I always believed him. Some nights when I lay awake in bed, I can feel the darkness peering in my window, stalking me in hopes of finishing the hunt from long ago.

Often Go Awry

*A letter from an unnamed church member,
hidden in the wall of a nearby village. Still unfound.*

An Urgent Notification for the Valentine Revival Ministry.

I am writing to you today to alert you of troubling news that I have just witnessed. I saw two policemen arresting Father Valentine on the edge of town. When I asked the lawman what he had done wrong, they told me to mind my own.

The Church is out for any member who might show compassion to him, and the whole town seems to have gone mad. I pray that you can make it here quickly to help make sure of a trial. Something dark has come over this town.

I fear for his life.

The Testimony

The following testimony was scribed from the memory of a young Paul Mathis.

January 10th, 1843

I do not wish to forget these words. They stay in my mind like a haunting. A cruel reminder of the wickedness that can come from my position. I write this now to not forget what I have heard, or to forget the tale of Thomas Edwin.

"I swear to tell the truth, so help me God."

"Can you describe your relationship with Father Gregory?"

"I can speak to the history of me and Father Gregory. I have met him many times in my while attending church and volunteering as a choir member."

"So you respected him?"

"I used to."

"What changed Mr. Edwin? What changed enough to make an attempt on his life?"

"He killed my son!"

"Let the record show that Mr. Edwin's son, Nathaniel, was not murdered by Father Gregory, and had no association with the death. As family and Mr. Edwin have previously stated, Nathaniel's death was a suicide. Confirmed by the local coroner. So Mr. Edwin, how is such a statement valid? Did this priest sitting in front of you tie the noose? Did he hang it around your son's neck? Did he tighten it around his neck? Did he push him off the bell tower of his school?"

"No he did not."

"Do you blame Father Gregory for the death of your son?"

"I do."

"Grief can make men do wicked things? Would you agree Mr. Edwin?"

"No, I would not."

"Puzzling. Mr. Edwin, the act of attempting to burn a man alive in his own house is not considered wicked in your eyes? If not that, what if that man was his family's priest, who baptized his son and spread the good word to his community. That is not considered wicked in your eyes?"

"No, I would not."

"Jury, please remember that Father Gregory is not on trial here. He is the defendant who was nearly killed as a result of Mr. Edwin's actions.

I ask these questions to gain an understanding of the motivation behind his actions and to determine whether he was justified in the eyes of the Lord and the rules of the law. Mr. Edwin, do you believe that your actions are justified?"

"I do."

"Could you please explain to myself, the judge and the jury how you came to the logic that Father Gregory was the murderer of your son although you have already admitted he had no hand in the act? How could you come to such a wild accusation? To such a deadly act?"

"I can. I was shocked by my son's sudden passing. I thought that I was the ideal father, that he had the ideal family. I tried my best, and wanted him to live life easier than mine. I thought he was happy and loved. I just wanted to know that. After his passing, neither I nor his mother had the strength to go into his room. I spoke with Father Gregory about my grief; this man of faith spoke to a father in mourning. He told me that my son was in hell, and that there was nothing I could do. That I must forget and only focus on my own salvation, and make sure my wife doesn't follow in his footsteps."

"Was it these remarks that caused your actions?"

"No, they were not. Although harsh I trusted him, he was a man of greater faith than I. So I believed his words and acted on them. I tried to focus less on my son and more on my work and my relationship with my wife. One day my son's room became just a room. I walked in with no remorse, and no memory of him. It was like discovering a new world. On his nightstand was a book, this little black book that he would write in from time to time. He always told me that he would be an author."

"Could you please tell me what any of this has to do with your motive?"

"Inside that book was a story, a story that turned a sunken man into a cold one. Inside, my son had written about his accounts with Father Gregory. That the priest had been abusing him. Forcing him to do disgusting acts for the sinful man."

"Libel, your honor!"

"It's not libel. My son was as honest as they came. He forced my son to engage in sexual acts against his will. He writes that the priest told him he was performing a service for the lord!"

"Honor, he is clearly making this up to justify his own wicked actions! We must strike this from the record."

"None of you might believe it, but I know it for certain. There was a feeling in the room that day. The feeling of a son being able to let go of his shame. He might not have tied the noose, but Father Gregory gave him the shame and a reason to jump."

"Your honor we cannot let this stand!"

As he was dragged out of the courtroom, Mr. Edwin continued to rant. The tears fell down his cheeks as he spoke and the anger of a justified man was at war with lies. I then realized that he was telling the truth.

"Father Gregory sent my son to hell for his own selfish reasons. Not for my son's sins, but for his. This man is no saint, and his only faith is that of a man who believes he will not be caught! Yes, I did lock you in your house and set it on fire! You deserve to die in hell on Earth, so I showed you a glimpse of it! Father, enjoy life while you can and let the guilt consume you. You will die one day, and hell will await you. Know, Father, that I will die smiling, knowing that I am righteous. While you die with worry and fear etched on your face!"

Please Lord, forgive me. I fear that I do not know the truth for certain. I worry that I might have sent a justified man to the gallows, while defending a monster. Is it sacrilegious to doubt a priest? I have faith in the Lord that you have led me to the correct decision, and that if not, you will give me the opportunity to correct it.

Dogma

PART THREE

THAT SMELL

*A text written on the inside page of a Holy Bible
in the fourth pew back of the Cathedral of Burryfield.
One of the few recovered items from the great fire.*

I've never been fond of,

The clothes they made me wear,

The meals they made me eat,

Money being borrowed and never returned,

Not being able to speak my mind,

Of not having meaning,

But most importantly I've never been fond of
that smell.

I've never been fond of that smell on that cold
ass day,

The smell of perfume and cigarettes,

The smell of coffee and homemade food.

The smell of an old wooden room filled with the laughter of familiar strangers.

I've never been fond of the day they married,

The day I saw a manipulative woman and self-serving man tie the knot,

The smell of lighter fluid and a lit cigarette combining,

In a wooden building built for the Lord.

I've never been fond of that smell.

A Reminder

<hr>

*A letter from Bishop Gregory to Judge Paul Mathis.
Used as a fire starter on a cold night.*

Judge Mathis,

It is with kind words I send you this message. As you are well aware, the Cathedral of Saint Burryfield has been damaged by the hands of a no good criminal named Valentine. It has been shared with me in private that you will be presiding over the case.

I find it quite fitting. Unfortunately for you and me, we both have experience with arson, and prosecuting it. I wish to remind you of the devastation this act has done to our community. I think a quick and prompt trial would be in the best interest of everyone. The case against him is as solid as one can be.

Remember when you first applied to be a judge of the court. It was the Church and myself who spoke graciously of your morality and church attendance. We used our influence to help ensure your position.

Although you have not attended as often as long ago and seem to be softer on people than I would like, I want to inform you that the Church still supports you.

We hope you will consider this history in the upcoming trial. We will be praying for God's will to be done.

Warm Regards,
Bishop Gregory of Burryfield

A Priest and a Jew Walk into a Bar

◆

A piece of mail lost to time. The ship carrying it sank in the Atlantic before it could be delivered.

SHALOM BROTHER,

How are you liking the new country? Are the people nice there? Are you fitting in? Our family misses you, and we hope to see you soon. Is there a synagogue there in Boston? Chana wishes to know if there is a thriving community there for us.

Chana and our kids are doing well, given the circumstances. A great fire has ravaged the forests we hunt in. Venison has been hard to get. The gentiles seem to have luck, but they do not prepare it properly. Azriel is growing into a respectable man, and Golda is the spitting image of her mother. Which I am glad for, but I fear I will be shooing off boys from our porch in the coming years.

I had an odd experience the other day, which in a weird way, reminded me of you. The other day at the local pub, I was sitting at the bar when a young man walked in. He was a priest for the bigger churches in our country. He had sorrow in his eyes. As you know, I find a way to talk to everyone, especially those in despair. I asked him what he was doing all the way in Ezra. He explained that he was part of a mission and that they were en route to Burryfield down south.

He drank vodka like you drank temple wine. His essence reminded me of a younger you. I asked him what they were to do in Burryfield. "We are to preach, and…" he stared at his empty glass with grief. "To help one of our own."

The cathedral there had been burned down a few days prior. He explained to me that the Church believes their traveling ministry was responsible. He told me that the Church wasn't a fan of their sermons. They had taken a priest into custody and that the trial would be starting sooner than expected.

Even after revealing this to me, the young man still looked distraught. Not as if he was upset about the cathedral or the righteous anger a man feels when blasphemy comes his way. He looked anxious, like a secret was tearing him up from within.

I asked him what was wrong, and he told me that the count who was paying for the ministry was giving him worries. "The man speaks the good word better than I ever could, yet he only does it at night. Few show up, and he will only do it occasionally. He is so heartbroken and defeated. He spoke to me one night and told me that he fears that he will never go to heaven, that his sins are too great. He tries to usher others to the divine treasure he cannot possess."

The young priest continued and pondered how he could be in the service of a man who thinks he is unredeemable. As it is a key piece to his faith and that he fears he is on the wrong side. It shocks me that these men of other faith still struggle with guilt as we do. It makes me wonder if YHWH created man to worry.

I told him the story father used to tell us. The one of the Hebrew Lycanthrope. A man of great Jewish faith who due to a hunting accident was turned into a werewolf. How he would have to cage himself once a month, to save himself from sin. Until one night, the beast breached the cage and went on to kill his neighbor's swine.

His guilt drove him mad, and he feared he had to escape to somewhere new. Far away from the memory. His faith so strong that he believed the one misstep of his kosher diet would displease YHWH. That he had failed in his eyes.

Man is tempted by yetzer hara. We all can go crazy sometimes due to hunger or temptation. We must embrace yetzer hatov. When shooting an arrow, we shall not dread on missing the bullseye, but continue and try to get closer to it. We cannot let dread or worry ruin our lives. Remember this, brother.

In the end, me and the priest discussed faith and grief and how it affects man. That sometimes the hardest internal struggles are forgiving ourselves when we go astray.

I hope to visit you soon and see how your life has improved. We are hoping that we will get to spend next Yom Kippur with you and that Chana can make her famous kugel. We are both so blessed to be married to such great women.

Shalom Aleichem

The Hearing

———◆———

*Scribbled in the pocketbook of a witness
of the trial of Father Valentine.*

Truly an odd series of events took place today.

Today I witnessed our local church and city going after a former priest from the Church. His proposed crime, setting the Cathedral on fire.

I never thought I would live to see the day that a priest was on trial for arson against his own Church.

The Bishop looked less like a holy man and more like an angry child. Always speaking out of turn. Although I cannot blame him too much, the case seemed pretty cut and dry to me.

The Church released a warning about the Valentine Ministry and how they are dangerous. They also privately dismissed Father Valentine from the church the same day. The son of the founder of the rival ministry. Then two days later, someone happens to set the cathedral on fire. It's not too hard to see the connection between these events. A simple act of retaliation from Valentine.

Although I cannot help but sympathize with the man, the daggers he received in that room, from the looks of the citizens, must cut deep into his heart. The guilt must be tearing him apart. For so many of his former members of his, Church that he gets sent to the gallows.

I have not seen anyone in the courtroom who has taken his side. His father has yet to show up in town, and no one from the Valentine Ministry has appeared in the crowds. However, it is always possible that they hide in fear of facing backlash from the Church or even being accused themselves.

Victor Peterson was arrested the other day for providing shelter to Valentine and not reporting him to the authorities. His trial is to follow soon after.

The trial is supposed to end tomorrow. The judge said to give his final verdict after closing arguments. Judge Mathis has always been a good man, in my opinion. He saw through the lies of my neighbor when he sold me a horse that was actually a mule.

What a truly remarkable day in the courts. I hope the trials of this town will continue to entertain me with further intrigue.

TO MY SON

◆

A letter that was burned in the post office.

DEAR NATHANIEL,

I hope things are going well for you at the academy. Your mother and I are quite proud of the man you have become. We eagerly await your arrival for Christmas. Your mother plans to fill you with enough food that you will keel over and die. She will be quite needy when you arrive, and I wish for you to be prepared for it. I know her compassion may be extreme but appreciate it when you can. She is not the young, energetic woman she was when I met her, and is starting to slow down in her old age.

I am preparing to do something tomorrow that might cause an uproar for our family when you return. I want you to be prepared for this as well.

I am currently hearing the merits of a case against a local priest. He is charged with the crime of burning down the cathedral in Burryfield. The Church has a strong case as to why they find this priest guilty of the crime. They had fired him before the act and had released a harsh statement against this priest's father. A simple case of retaliation is their main argument.

They also have a few witnesses that state they saw this priest start the fire. The priest has no alibi or credible witnesses to confirm his side of events as he claims to be asleep during the time.

It seems pretty cut and dry. The town and the Church are expecting me to find him guilty. They want me to give him the death penalty. It is the only course of action that will calm their anger and retain their faith in me as a judge.

Unfortunately, I cannot give the verdict they wish. A feeling has grasped my mind and heart. I do not know if it's my usual intuition from many years of this profession, or divine intervention. Maybe a bit of both. I believe this priest's defense. I do not think he is guilty of this act. I think the Church has created many enemies throughout the years. It is no secret to our family that I have a mistrust of Bishop Gregory. That I travel to the parishes for service, instead of the Cathedral that is closer to our residence.

The Bishop has had several cases against him in the past years. Since I defended him once long ago though, I am not allowed to be the Judge in any case if he is the plaintiff or defendant. Since this case is technically the Church board against the priest, a gray area is presented where I have the ability to see him in my court.

When I looked into his eyes today, I saw the same look of arrogance that was on his face that fateful day. I'm still unsure that I made the right choices back then. I was a younger man like you are now. So worried about establishing my career that I cared less about the truth and more about how many cases I won. I hope you can learn a lesson from my mistakes on this. Honor, after all, is more important than any money the world will promise you.

I fear that I know the true culprit of this crime. I can't be certain, and I have my reservations about it. As you know, I am a realist, and have never believed in ghost stories. I do believe though that a ghost might have been responsible for the fire. Thomas Edwin, who I helped send to the gallows so many years ago. I believe he is responsible for the fire. That he couldn't find peace in the afterlife until he got back at the bishop.

I know I must seem like I have lost my wits. I am not certain that it is a literal ghost that caused the fire, perhaps though it is a figurative ghost.

That the crimes of the bishop have led to this. I may not know who started that fire, but I believe whoever did it was justified in their actions.

So tomorrow at the trial, I will give my final verdict of not guilty. I do not expect it to go over well with the community or Church. For a while, the town might be spiteful towards our family. We might not be invited to as many social events, which will bring much comfort to you and me. Disdain to your mother, no doubt.

I have given this decision much thought and did not come to it rashly. I always knew I would eventually be presented with an opportunity by the Lord to correct my past errors. I believe this is that. It might cost me my career and trust in the community, but I know it is the right thing to do either way. I'll enjoy an early retirement as a shut-in. I'll get to spend more time with your mother and be a more attentive father to you.

Son, the profession you are setting out into can turn men cold and jaded. It can also inflate their ego and make them feel like a god. Remember, there is only one true God. Remember to always do what's right. I trust that you will.

Stay safe at the academy and learn as much as you can. I know you might not think about it now, but one day you will miss it. Your mother and I send encouragement and love.

Sincerely, a Proud Father

TO MY FATHER

◆

A prayer heard in Burryfield on a cold,
restless night.

Our Father,
Who art in Heaven,
-

Behold me at thy feet,
O Jesus of Nazareth,
Behold the most wretched of creatures,
Who comes into Thy presence humbled and
penitent?
Have mercy on me,
O Lord,
According to Thy great mercy.
I have sinned, and my sins are always before thee.
Yet my soul belongs to thee,
For thou hast created it,
And redeemed it with thy precious blood.
Ah, grant that thy redeeming work be not in
vain.

Have pity on me;
Give me tears of true repentance;
Pardon me as thou didst pardon the penitent
thief;
Look upon me from thy throne in heaven and
give me thy blessing.
I believe in God,

-

Amen.

No Good Deed
Goes Unpunished

◆

The final words of Eli Crosby.

"If you wish to make a final statement, this is the time to do it."

"I wish I never stepped into that courtroom that day. I was pretty heated. We all were! Doesn't excuse my actions though. I know that. We were all so certain about that trial. There wasn't one person there who didn't think he was guilty. Nevertheless, I still caused a scene and caused that fatal accident.

I'm so sorry for the family. For taking him from you. It wasn't my place. I took him too early, and I apologize. It's not like me to act like that. The night prior, I was at the pub, and we were all talking about it. It riled me up. This man sitting in the shadow of the corner kept daring me to do it as he smoked his cigar.

I don't know what brought that out in me. Something deep inside me awakened. I am guilty of my actions. I pray. I pray that none of you will have to deal with this great evil. It only tears me up inside with regret and sorrow.

It was a mistake that I killed that man. I had malice in my heart when I walked in there. Even if he wasn't the one I intended, I went in there looking to leave with blood on my hands.

To his wife and son, I apologize deeply. I know I'm rambling. I know I'm repeating.

I just –

It's hard to come up with your last words. I just want to bring proper closure to you, Nathaniel. I lost my father to a drunken fight in an alley. I wondered what they squabbled about to this day. What was so worth it to give up his life?

Just know that I had no ill will towards your father. He was a good man and a good judge. I thought I could be my own executioner, and serve the will of God as I saw fit.

In the end, I was just as corrupt as he is. I'm sorry.

Dear Lord, please forgive me."

Tragedy Strikes Burryfield Courthouse

---

*The front page story of the Burryfield Chronicle
on the first day of fall.*

An awful turn of events took place yesterday in the Burryfield courtroom. Judge Paul Mathis was shot and killed in the middle of the court, and Johnathan Valentine was wounded. The culprit has been identified as Eli Crosby, a local blacksmith. Crosby has been taken into police custody and has been charged with manslaughter.

From several eyewitness accounts, Crosby pulled a revolver out of his coat and aimed it at Father Valentine as he was taking his seat. A few men in the crowd rushed to tackle Crosby, and during the scuffle, Crosby let off one shot. Johnathan Valentine was struck in his shoulder, and the bullet continued to hit Judge Mathis fatally in the head, leaving spectators in disbelief.

Johnathan Valentine, who was on trial for the burning of the Burryfield Cathedral, was rushed to St. Burryfield hospital to be treated. His condition has been described as stable by the Burryfield inspector. "Mister Valentine will be held at the hospital for further care; once the hospital finds him in better spirits, he will return to his jail cell until the trial is finished."

Judge Paul Mathis' death has resulted in the trial being pushed back until a new judge can be found to take his place. Paul Mathis served as the lead judge of Burryfield for the last thirty years. Before that, he served as a public defender for the community. Mayor Wallace has announced that he would personally pay for all funeral expenses.

"It's been a rough few weeks for the people of Burryfield. Some of our finest institutions have been attacked, and many people are distressed and angry. I urge all citizens to remember the events at the courthouse today, and how one's anger can do more damage than intended." Mayor Wallace would not answer any questions about the trial, stating, "I have just lost a great friend. He was the only one able to make that decision. He was truly a noble man who would have made the right decision."

Judge Mathis was set to give his final verdict on the trial before the tragedy. Many legal scholars and community members were expecting a guilty sentence, and were awaiting to see if the judge would award a death sentence to Valentine.

The Mathis family has requested privacy during this time. Mayor Wallace has also issued a statement to the public asking that the public respect the wishes of the Mathis family. "Although a very shocking tragedy has taken place to a respected public figure, this is still very much a private affair for his family. People who saw him less as a judge and more as their loving husband and father."

The funeral for Judge Paul Mathis has no scheduled date as of the time of publication. Mayor Wallace is expected to announce plans in the coming days.

Juniper Estate to Burryfield

<hr>

*A conversation between Father Reynolds
and a stranger on a train.*

"What book are you reading?"

"The holy bible. Are you familiar with the good word?"

"I mean, what book in the bible?"

"Matthew."

-

"And whoever says, you fool! Should be guilty enough to go into the fiery flame."

"You are quite knowledgeable of your bible verses."

"There used to be a time when almost every man was knowledgeable in them. Alas though, it seems we dive deeper into darkness every day."

"Well said."

"What organization do you belong to? Protestant, Lutheran, Catholic?"

"The Church, but currently, I'm providing services with the Count Valentine ministry."

"Oh really? I've heard quite troubling things about that man?"

"Well, I can assure you I have only seen good come from my work so far."

"Is it true what they say?"

"What's that?"

"That he's a vampire? A strigoi?"

"I believe that is just some gossip spread by those who do not support us?"

"I heard he sold his soul to the devil."

"Where did you hear such a thing? Burryfield Gazette?"

"A reliable source. He said he feeds on the blood of man too."

"Well, I have not seen such behavior. I haven't seen much of the man you speak of, in fact. All I know for sure is that he wishes to spread the word of God. I'm willing to stand by any man who can do that."

"Ah, a respectable man, you are Father."

"Are you a member of a specific church?"

"No, I am not. Not anymore."

"What changed, if you don't mind me asking?"

"Oh, it was so long ago. Who could remember such a thing?"

"Most people who lose their faith often experience a tragedy. I do not wish to make you uncomfortable or bring back any bad memories."

"Father, you are not making me uncomfortable. No such tragedy has happened to me. I guess I just didn't find it worth it."

"What do you mean it's not worth it? I don't understand."

"You are a young man, it will come with time."

"I can't be much younger than you."

"Your words are too kind. I look younger than I am. I live a carefree life. No worries to age me sooner than needed."

"So one day, you just decided that salvation was not worth it?"

"Precisely."

"I'm sorry if I look shocked or too simple, I just don't quite understand. "

"Let me try to explain it better for you then. When I was a follower of Christ, I had to follow all these rules. I had to care about individuals and try to help them. Selfless service

is what I think you call it now. But once I gave it up, I was free. No longer shackled by any restriction. I am free to choose what I want my destiny to be."

"But this life is only temporary, and our actions here determine if we will see eternal life."

"Everyone talks about eternal life like it's some fucking prize. Now I get to live for eternity with no purpose, oh, what a gracious God."

"That is a pessimistic outlook on the afterlife."

"I guess it is Father Reynolds."

"How do you know my name?"

"You introduced yourself to the woman who got off at the last stop. The pretty redhead with a prominent chest."

"I beg your pardon, but I will not make a conversation with a man who talks so poorly of a woman."

"My bad Father, my bad."

"Father?"

"I said I do not wish to talk with you anymore."

"But I am a sinner in need of redemption."

"You have stated that you do not believe in the faith anymore."

"Oh that is true father, but you do."

"Are you coming to me for confession?"

"I do not want your forgiveness. Just a conversation."

"Are you genuinely interested in being forgiven?"

"No, I am not Father. But you are. You believe that anyone can be saved. Is that not right?"

"Everyone can be saved. That is why Jesus died for our sins."

"You seem frazzled Father. I have heard better arguments on faith from toddlers."

"What is it that you want from me? A discussion of faith or to badger me about mine?"

"Father, do you believe that anyone can be saved? No matter what evil they have committed in this world? A clean slate for every rapist and child molester, just if they pray to God on their knees and say they are sorry?"

"If they truly seek repentance, yes. It might seem cruel, and it does not mean they won't have to pay for their actions on this plane. But I do believe God will let them into the gates of heaven."

"So I could go to heaven? Even though I have done such wicked deeds."

"You can, you truly can. Salvation is something not to be taken with such disdain as you have applied to it."

"Father, will you help me in my repentance to God?"

"It would be my honor. Take your time with your confession, do not be afraid of guilt or humility. I have heard it all."

"Oh Father, I have sinned. I have killed so many men. I have ripped out their hearts and feasted on their fear. I have bathed in the blood of families and made love to their sons and daughters. I have diverted people from you, oh so gracious king almighty. I have disemboweled innocent children from within, and then smiled with glee over their corpses in front of their screaming parents. I have swallowed babies whole and looked into the face of an innocent, scared girl as I deflowered her while wearing the skin of her father. As he screams on the floor in pain and horror as he watches his daughter enjoying it. Oh Lord, I have promised so many things to so many people and never came through. I have whispered doubt into the ears of thousands. I have shoved anxiety and lust down their throats in the hope of pleasuring myself. I have poisoned communions and tainted sermons. All for the sole purpose of ruining your grand scheme. To consume these souls as my own, to grow more powerful in my freedom of you.

Your graciousness is your biggest weakness. Not able to disown me yet, due to the fact that you think I may come around. The hopeful tyrant you are! You want me to say sorry for all these deeds. Oh lord, I'm so sorry for my actions. Will you please forgive me? Pretty please? Pretty, pretty please?"

"Do you think he forgave me, Father?"

"I do not know what to say."

"It's impressive, isn't it? The graciousness of God?"

"Who are you?"

"How rude of me not to introduce myself; my name is Leopold. I'm the man who is here to drive you farther from God."

"That is not possible. Nothing can do that. You are merely a mad man who wishes to confuse others."

"Are you sure about that? For starters, do you think he forgave me, father?"

"I'm not sure. It's only for him to decide."

"That's a nice way of saying no."

"If you were truly sorry —"

"I'm not sorry about anything. You could tell by my tone I wasn't sincere. I don't need to be sorry for anything. I have no shame. Unlike you."

"What are you talking about?"

"You have sins that you regret."

"Of course I do; I'm a sinner inherently. I must strive to be better though, and it is through the Lord I can do that."

"So you feel bad for the sins you have committed and have truly repented them?"

"Yes!"

"You don't feel joy when thinking about them?"

"No, I do not!"

"Oh, Father, do not lie."

"I am not lying."

"I know you are Father. You still grin when you think about breaking Mathias's arm. Why wouldn't you? He deserved it. Stealing the girl you wanted to marry."

"How do you know about my bro –"

"Rosaline was also a redhead with big bouncy breasts. It seems you have a type, Father."

"Do not speak about her that way!"

"It's not like you don't think about her that way. You often have dreams about her naked body. How you would use her to your heart's delight. How many times have you pleasured yourselves to those thoughts?"

"How do you know? Stop this!"

"What if I don't stop? What will you do? Are you going to forgive me or are you going to break my arm?"

"You are a mad man! I will not be swept into your sinful thinking!"

"Father? What if I can give you something that God can't?"

"You can't give me anything that God can't deli –"

"Rosaline?"

"Now I have your attention. Rosaline is pregnant with a child, right? A baby girl whose father is supposed to be Mathias. Although I could change that?"

"How?"

"Secret. Sorry."

"I don't believe you."

"Oh, you with so little faith."

"You're lying, and trying to deceive me."

"If you are willing to give up your soul to me, and let go of your faith of salvation. Then I will make it so that you were wed to Rosaline and father to her expecting child?"

"No. She is happy with him, and I am happy with how things are."

"I see. There is no way to change that, I suppose. What if that woman from earlier

came back, the one that reminded you of her? Would you like her instead?"

"You cannot do that. You are a man, a deceiving man with a cunning tongue and nothing more."

"If you need me to prove it to you then all you had to do was ask nicely. Don't play so hard to get Father. I'll bring more than just one this time; that way, you can pick one or two."

"How are you doing this?"

"Doing what, Father? I am just a man with a cunning tongue."

"HELLO MISTER REYNOLDS."

"You are not real!"

"WE ALL WANT YOU MISTER REYNOLDS."

"I declared myself celibate many years ago!"

"Show him the goods ladies!"

"WE'LL UNDRESS FOR YOU MISTER REYNOLDS."

"No! Stop! Cover yourselves!"

"DO YOU LIKE OUR BIG CHESTS MISTER REYNOLDS?"

"Open your eyes Father. They are here for you."

"I do not believe this. I am dreaming."

"LET US PLEASURE YOU MISTER REYNOLDS. LET US FUCK YOU!"

"Maybe you are, Father. Maybe you will wake up from your train ride at your stop in Burryfield. Relieved that this is all over; that I am merely a figment of your imagination. What a dark and sinful imagination you must have. A naughty one at that. When you wake up Father, tell Valentine I say hello. He is a good friend of mine."

There Will Be Blood

PART FOUR

THE GIFT OF THE WATER

A poem written by Count Valentine.
Kept in his breast pocket.

Water,
A gift that delivers us from sin.
Water,
A gift that puts out the flame.
Water,
A gift that grows our grain.
Water,
A gift that cleans us.
Water,
A gift that brought me my son.
Water,
A gift that gives me purpose.
Water,
Be thankful for water.

CLOSING ARGUMENTS

Court transcript of the closing arguments in the case of the Church of Burryfield vs Johnathan Valentine.

Judge Harker: The court will now hear the closing arguments of the Church, followed by the closing argument of Johnathan Valentine. Then we will all return to our homes to get a good night's rest and I will consider the arguments of the case for my final verdict tomorrow. Mister Kingston, are you ready to proceed?

Mister Kingston: We are your honor.

Judge Harker: The floor is yours.

Mister Kingston: Ladies and gentlemen in attendance, I wish to make it known today that revenge is not the proper response to anger. Revenge is the enemy of justice and the truth. Man cannot be the determiner of these things. Only God can be. Burryfield, the town we stand in today, is built on these principles. Saint Burryfield fought against the revenge of our enemies. It was he who fought the lies of the Greeks when they tried to take our land. His truth could not be defeated in argument. For where one has truth, they also have God.

I come today bearing the truth. Mister Valentine has already admitted that he felt angry about being forced to leave the Church. Church documents show a record of infractions due to a short temper during his time as a holy man! Mister Valentine has no alibi or witness for his whereabouts the night of the fire. He hid from the authorities for several days before trying to make a run for the hills in the blackness of night. Are these the acts of an innocent man?

Last week we saw the tragedy and pain that can be caused by revenge, when someone decides to take justice into their own hands. Not allowing the court or the almighty himself to serve it fairly and just. I submit to you today that the burning of the Cathedral was another tragedy caused by the work of revenge. This is the truth.

Your honor, I request you to see this truth and punish this deed with the punishment it deserves. There is no reason that a righteous, honorable judge should be dead while a guilty and vengeful man continues to breathe. Thank you, your honor.

Judge Harker: The prosecution has now spoken. Its argument has been received, and now we will move on to the defense. Mister Valentine, I understand that you wish to represent yourself in the closing argument. Is this true?

Johnathan Valentine: It is your honor.

Judge Harker: Very well, you may begin your final argument.

Johnathan Valentine: Thank you, your honor. I come before this crowd today knowing that I will not be able to change your mind. In the eyes of the Church, I am guilty, while in the eyes of the Lord, I am innocent. I did not burn the cathedral. A point I'm sure you will all disagree on. Instead of trying to convince you, I have decided that I would rather take what time I have to do what I have loved most. Spreading the gospel. If you will join me in prayer.

Father, who art in Heaven, blessed by thy name. I come before you in shame, for I am a sinner, as we all are. I ask you to breathe clarity into this courtroom today, and to let your will be done. Lord, I ask for forgiveness for my past sins. I wish to die a humble man, Lord. Let my death have meaning. Let me have the will to continue on in my honesty until my final breath. Lord forgive them, for they do not know what they are doing. In the name of the Father, Son and the Holy Ghost. Amen.

Judge Harker: With that prayer, the arguments of this case are now finished. I thank you all for your time and patience with this case. I will return tomorrow morning with my final verdict. As for all of you, I pray for a good night's sleep and lovely rest of your day. Court adjourned.

Arrival

<hr>

The Count, Father Grisham, and I have arrived in Burryfield this afternoon. Father Reynolds is expected later tonight by train. Deacon Christianson is expected in the early morning. Travel was rough, but our early departure from our mission was a success. We have made it in time for the trial. Father Grisham is on his way into town to see about an opportunity for the Mission to speak on behalf of Father Valentine before the final verdict.

The Count's irritation has only grown in our travels. His worry for his son has left him fighting with ancient demons within himself. I fear what might happen in the event of a death sentence tomorrow. I do not wish for his good reputation to be sullied by an aggressive act of retaliation. No matter how justified it must be. It will only leave the town painting him as the figure they believe him to be.

Burryfield is not the same since I last saw it. The city continues to grow and grow. The fields I ran in as a child are now a distant memory. The city extends into the woods nearby. The skyline haunts me, as the void in the sky sends a shiver down my spine. Although, I have seen several cases of true evil while in the Count's employ, its rawness still shocks me.

Our numbers have continued to dwindle. Two priests decided to disembark when we decided to leave for Burryfield early. That's not counting the ministry's size being cut in half once the Church deemed us dangerous to the public. Even with all the money we can promise, no priest wishes to be associated with us.

-

Father Grisham came back with painful news. The city has stated that the mission is not allowed to speak. Count Valentine was given a formal warning to leave town, and that if any one associated with the revival was seen at the court, they would be arrested immediately.

The Count has walked into the forest to spend the night alone. I'm sure some poor tree will feel his wrath. All of us had to find camp outdoors tonight. Father Grisham has headed to the train depot to alert Father Reynolds, in hopes of getting him out safely.

Lord, I do not know what tribulations await us in the coming days. I pray for your guidance and forgiveness. Send your angels to watch over us.

Flowers for Helen

Another undelivered letter, from a long-lost love.

Dear Helen,

I visited you tonight. I cleaned off the lot and sat next to you. I didn't cry this time. I knew you wouldn't want that. I arrived in the city today. It's not the small farming village you knew it as. It's expanded to the size of Rome. It's a religious destination. The Church has expanded exponentially across our country. I hope I have helped in some way.

The leaders of the Church in Burryfield don't seem to like us much. Hornsworth tells me it's because they are afraid of outsiders, and that the competition we present is seen as a threat. I don't understand how there is any competition. We both have the same goal of sharing the word of God. Providing help to those in need and creating a place where faith can thrive. Maybe they're afraid of us taking tidings from their commission plates. However, I have assured the Bishop that we do not collect a tithe.

I fear that it is bad luck that always follows me. God is punishing me for my wicked deeds. I can always hear you whispering in my ear at night, telling me that I have to forgive myself. I say that if one does truly forgive themselves, one can strive to be better. Then God will forgive them when they repent. My sins are unforgivable.

God may be gracious, but I don't know if I can be with myself. A sinner like me does not belong in heaven. I swear I would take my life if it didn't mean I would lose you. You will be the closest thing to Heaven I will have ever known. So, for now, I will continue to help spread the word, and still have you in my heart.

My son is on trial. The Church here has accused him of burning down their cathedral. The son I raised wouldn't have done such a thing. I was too much of a good example of a bad example. He saw how sin could cause a man to wither away. He has always been a righteous man. A great priest and friend to all who know him. He doesn't deserve this. I feel like he is serving my penance for the sins of the past.

I have faith, though, that he won't be found guilty. There is no evidence that he was there, just a motive. A motive that anyone who has anger against the Church could have. The judge in this trial has a record of being fair. He's a strong man, and I don't think the Church would have the power to bully him. I just pray my son is not worried. He has been known to worry too much, I guess that is one thing I did pass on to him.

I wish you could have met him, my love. He reminds me a lot of you. His faith is strong, and his temper is mild. He cares for others more than himself. I hope you don't meet him sooner than attended. I would hate to be separated from another loved one for eternity.

Love, I wish you the best. I miss you more and more each day. My love has never wavered. Not in all this time. You were the only one for me. Until next time.

With a full heart, your grateful fool

A Fireside Chat

———◆———

The memories of a tree from a dark and cold night,
where its last night was spent as firewood.

"Valentine? Count Valentine? Is that you?"

"Who's there? Who calls for me?"

"It's Father Reynolds! I arrived in Burryfield. I was told of the news of the hearing tomorrow."

"And so of it?"

"I've come to check on you. To make sure you are alright."

"I'll be fine, Father. Go and rest. There is an emotional day waiting for us tomorrow."

"Valentine! Something happened on the train. Something I think you should know about."

"It can wait until tomorrow. Get some rest, Father."

"Please! I will not be able to sleep until I share this with you."

"If you find it that urgent, I must hear from you. Come closer, Father. Warm up next to the fire."

"So what's troubling you, Father?"

"Tonight on the train. There was this, this man. He was so evil. He coaxed me into this despicable conversation. He knew things about me he couldn't have possibly known. It was like I was living through a nightmare."

"I have heard similar stories. The priests I have employed have often been threatened by a stranger in the night. When one is doing the work of God, then Lucifer will try his hardest to prevent it. Before Moses was born, Lucifer used his influence on man to cause the Egyptian people to kill any Hebrew son born in their land. God preserves though, and because of the mother's faith, she sent her son into a river in a basket. Faith let her know he would be safe."

"Count Valentine, can I ask you a question?"

"Let me guess. You wish to request to return home. You wouldn't be the first, and I unders —"

"No, Count Valentine, that is not what I want to ask. I am aware that there will be troubles and grief from my line of work."

"Then what is your question, Father?"

"Are you a vampire?"

"Ha! Haha, no I am not. Haha! Ha!"

"I hope I have not offended you."

"Oh no. Ha! Just amused me is all. Who told you that?"

"Just rumors around town. Things said about you by those who speak ill of our ministry."

"And you believed them?"

"Not at first. I must confess, though, that I have noticed some oddities in your behavior that could lead one to hold such a suspicion."

"Ha! Please tell me, Father, of these."

"Well, you seem to only be awake at night. You hide your face in the darkness, even now. You don't perform any baptisms, and there have been reports of you drinking blood from wild animals?"

"There are also reports that I burnt down the Saint Burryfield Cathedral. Do not believe in such rumors. As for the others, I do have my reasons. I can say, though, that I am not a vampire. Do you know what a vampire means?"

"Isn't it a creature of the night with fangs and pointy ears? That lives for eternity as long as it feeds on the blood of virgins?"

"I guess in a way, that is accurate. That is the way most people see it now. Originally,

it was a loved one of a family member who had returned from the grave to cause mischief and death. I am not one of these. However, I do suspect that our ministry has had its run-ins with them. Perhaps even you on the train tonight."

"So why do you hide yourself?"

"Shame, mostly."

"What is there to be ashamed of?"

"I have committed sins in my life. Sins that can never be redeemed."

"You sound just like the man on the train. Although you are remorseful of your actions."

"Remorse is all it seems I have to these days."

"What could cause such shame that you hide your face?"

"It would be best to show you."

-

"You are so young!"

"In appearances only, I'm afraid."

"How could you be the father to Father Valentine? You look younger than he is."

"I can assure you it is a cruel deception."

"So you are not his father?"

"I am his father. I raised him as my own and love him with the love only a parent can have for a child."

"Who is his mother?"

"I don't know. I found him in a river one day. I had prayed to God to give me a purpose. Send me a sign on how I can try to redeem myself. Then it happened. I heard the cry of an infant. I saw him floating down the river in a crib. I went out into the river to save him. I then searched for hours, looking for the parents. After a month of looking, I figured the worst. I took him as my own. I gave him my last name and gave him everything I could. He never asked for much. He is a good and simple man."

"How is it that you look so young then?"

"It's a very long story. Not sure I could explain it easily. Or that you would believe me."

"We have plenty of night left before morning. I would like to know the man I'm serving better."

"Well, the man you are serving is God; you are not serving me. I am paying you for your hard work and make sure you are fed and not worrying about your family's finances".

"Well, if I'm risking my reputation with the Church, I would like to know more about you, Valentine?"

"Are you afraid that I am a swindler, Father?"

"I just want to know your intentions are pure."

"My intentions are as pure as they can be. I would swear on my child's life."

"Something else happened on the train. The stranger told me to say hello on his behalf. He said his name was Leopold."

"Did you just say Leopold?"

"Yes, he said he was a friend of yours."

"What else did he say?"

"He said you sold your soul to the devil long ago. That he would let me be wed to the woman I love if I gave him my soul."

"What did you say?"

"I said no. I didn't trust him. I couldn't be with her for a reason."

"I'm sure he did more than just tell you. His hypnosis is very strong. It takes a man of strong will to resist his tricks. You are a good man, Father Reynolds."

"How did you know this man?"

"At one point in my life, I considered him a friend. That was a long time ago, though. Back when I was like him. Men like me and him, we could never be saved. God is gracious enough to do it, but we don't deserve it."

"Long ago, Leopold and I were priests together. Both of us were young and excited to go out on missions. To spread the word of God and his son Jesus Christ, to those who have never heard it before. That was a few generations ago. People weren't as kind to us back then. They were skeptical of the messiah. We were being persecuted and arrested for our beliefs. Leopold and I were fearless, though. We had faith that God was on our side. That was before. Before we saw the body, he was meant to lead the Church. Protected by God. Then we saw him, crucified upside down. At that point in our lives it was our first glimpse of the act. How cruel it was to a man and his spirit. Peter was what we strived to be; was this what was waiting for us?"

"Are you telling me that you witnessed the crucifixion of Peter, the apostle?"

"I know it sounds ridiculous. Unfortunately, it is true. I wept for weeks. Leopold was never the same after that day."

-

"One night, we were walking to Rome when a figure approached us. It was dark, and we couldn't see it well. He asked if everything was okay and if we needed help. His words are still carved in my brain. He showed us that he was not human with acts of "wonder". All deceptions. He told us that we could have whatever we wanted in exchange for a fee. I wish I could blame it on a young man's stupidity for getting me to agree. Unfortunately, my envy got the better of me. Leopold desired strength in order to perform the same miracles. He desired to defend himself. He was terrified. He was given our souls in exchange for our wishes. Although with all deals that sound too good, there were consequences. Since we have no souls, we couldn't age. Death couldn't come to us, only if self-inflicted or from the blade of each other. If so, we were to be sent to his realm, away from God. No matter of repentance could change it. Over the years, Leopold realized he could become even stronger if he tricked people into giving him their souls. He could never grant their wishes, he could convince them that he could though. That brings us to today. I try to follow his trail of misdeeds. Bringing hope to those who have been hurt. Leading them to a treasure I cannot possess."

"What is it that you wanted?"

"A woman. Her uncle was a king back then. She was a noble that could not marry a commoner like me. I would sneak letters to her as a boy. She would write back. It was my

first love. He told me that he could change the king's mind. I wasn't a strong man like you. I gave in. Unfortunately, she grew old and eventually died. She was a magnificent woman, she is in heaven now. I know I will never get to see her again."

"Why do you say that?"

"Because I am not allowed in heaven. I've been too wicked. I gave my soul to the devil, and when she died. I couldn't handle that pain. Knowing I would never see her again. Darkness surrounded me, and I consumed it like a starving man. I was just as bad as Leopold. He was doing it for the amusement of it. I was doing it for my hatred towards God. I have lived lifetimes as a monster. Straying man from God, causing them pain to deepen the wedge. I killed children and priests to leave people without hope. I became an evil so great that demons themselves envied my skill. I don't deserve heaven after that."

"Have you repented?"

"No."

"Don't you want forgiveness?"

"I don't deserve it."

"Count Valentine. What changed? What made you turn towards a life of spreading the gospel?"

"Anger can only last for so long. It slowly dwindled year by year, until there was no more. Then one day, I saw this child, a boy crying over his mother's body. Eventually, he stopped crying. He carried her to the woods all by himself. I watched as he buried her, collected flowers from the nearby fields and laid a wreath on the disturbed soil. He then continued on. Working the field, and taking care of his siblings. There was such goodness in this child. I don't know why it changed my mind for sure. Maybe his perseverance inspired me. I prayed to God for help, for a purpose. That's when I became a father, and my son was so fascinated with the faith. Like me when I was a boy. He relit that old flame inside of me. I took my fortune and started employing priests for my ministries. Hoping that I could somehow make amends for my past actions. It's not enough, though. I still need to do more."

"Valentine. I don't believe that you are a monster. I believe that only you perceive yourself that way. You can still repent, and be right in the eyes of the Lord. That's more important than where your soul goes."

"I'll work on it Father, and maybe one day I can forgive myself enough to truly repent to God."

The Verdict

A speech read by Judge Harker.

Ladies and gentleman of Burryfield,

I would once again like to thank you for your patience during these past weeks and this trial. I do not wish to test it any further. I will now begin to read my final verdicts in the case of the Church of Burryfield vs Johnathan Valentine. For the account of arson to the Cathedral of Saint Burryfield, I find you guilty. I have thought good and hard about the sentence. I do not like sending men to the gallows, but in your case, I'm afraid I have no other options. Johnathan Valentine is to be hanged tomorrow at noon. He will be joined by Victor Peterson and Eli Crosby. May God have mercy on their souls.

Now that the trial is over, and my final verdict has been recorded. I would like to speak publicly to the crowd here today. In all my years as a judge and as a lawyer, I have not seen the acts of one man cause so much trouble to a community. I hope with my verdict today, I have eased the sorrow of the community and that we can move on stronger than before. I feel that Judge Mathis would have made the same verdict. He was a man of great faith, and he would not have let this sacrilege stand.

Ladies and gentlemen, I bid you adieu.

Scribbled in a Cell

*The following note is carved into the wooden
door of the abandoned Burryfield jail.*

Tomorrow I will join them.
All those who have perished in the cause.
The martyrs and their savior.
I do not know why God had planned this for
me.
I hope it brings peace to those who need it.
Let my death bring others to God.
Salvation is possible for any man.
No matter his sin.
Let God accept them into his arms and say.
"You are forgiven, my child."

The Wallace Speech

———◆———

Mayor Wallace's speech to the people of Burryfield.
The day three men were set to be hanged.

Today will be a historic day for our city. A day
that will be remembered by all in attendance. A
day the Church of our town will never forget.

It is important that today is stained into our
memories. A reminder of the cruelty of man.
That even the best of us can fall if we act too
hastily. Most importantly a reminder that there is
justice in this town. That malice will not prevail
in Burryfield for long. That you will always have
to pay for your actions.

Standing before you today are three men.
A priest, a blacksmith, and a local farmer. Men
who weeks ago were upstanding members of
Burryfield. It will be hard to remember that
as their reputations have been stained with sin

and tragedy. Their names will evoke horror and sadness for years to come.

Johnathan Valentine has been found guilty of the act of arson. The fire he started resulted in the destruction of Saint Burryfield Cathedral. A religious landmark for the Church and the greater community. Valentine's act was a threat to our established Church and the values of the people of Burryfield.

Victor Peterson was a local farmer who would attend mass every Sunday. He was a man revered for his humbleness and kindness. He is now found guilty as a conspirator in the burning of the Cathedral. Aiding in hiding a fugitive and helping him try to escape. Peterson's actions are a cruel reminder of the consequences for those who promote malicious intent; who harbor evilness for power.

Eli Crosby was a talented blacksmith whose skills could not be matched in this city or the country. He is known for his calm manner and donations to the Church. Unfortunately, due to an uncontrollable and reckless rage, he now finds himself with the title of a murderer. His vigilantism resulted in the death of the honorable Judge Mathis. A man who served this town well and asked nothing for it.

These three men are all examples. Examples of what rash thinking and spiteful actions can do to an innocent person. An innocent family or community. Let us not look on this day with victory or malice. Let it remind us for the rest of our lives, that sin is a constant enemy. A battle we must face day by day. That we must always look out for those around us and not be selfish in our actions. I pray that you and your families are safe, and that no more harm will come to our blessed town.

Cut Short

◆

"Victor Peterson, you are about to be sentenced to death. If you wish to make a final statement, this is the time to do it."

"I do not regret my actions. I feel that I served the Lord as best I could. I do not understand why the Lord has planned my life in this way. I am thankful that I will soon get to see my dear wife again. Please remember me by who I am. The man I was. Not this picture they're pointing me out to be. But a man who worked hard and helped his fellow man. A man who gave his earnings to the Church and oath to God. I do not in any way think that I was a perfect man. I'm a sinner like anyone here. If this is God's punishment for me, I will take it with grace.

As a final act of faith in my Lord. Let the meek inherit the kingdom of heaven."

"For the act of arson that caused the destruction of the cathedral and for oaths, you have broken to your Church and its members. Johnathan Valentine, you are about to be sentenced to death. If you wish to make a final statement, this is the time to do it."

"I have only one thing to say. The Lord w —"

Silence

PART FIVE

The Legend of Saint Burryfield

---◆---

A description found on a marble sculpture of Saint Burryfield, found in the Cathedral of Burryfield today.

SAINT BURRYFIELD 1553
PATRON SAINT OF FAITH

Saint Burryfield was named after his father's land. It was the only name he knew when he first joined the Church at 16. He became ordained as a priest only five years later. He spent his time traveling with ministries across Europe. There have been many accounts of Saint Burryfield healing a wounded child with a prayer to Jesus.

His most notable anecdote was that of the fire in the valley. A small village that Saint Burryfield's mission was helping came under attack by their warring neighbors. They set fire around the area, leaving the village to burn with innocent people inside. While many people from the village and mission ran in fear, Saint Burryfield stood fast, helping the villagers. Huddled in a circle, Saint Burryfield prayed to God for protection. His faith in the rescue is said to have stopped the fire in its tracks. Sending it in the opposite direction towards the attackers.

The surviving villagers rebuilt their village into a thriving city with the help of the Church. Renaming the city to Burryfield in honor of the man who once saved them.

Saint Burryfield was officially canonized in 1603 by the Church. A cathedral was commissioned in 1624. A beacon for the Church in the east. Standing tall, it reminds us of Saint Burryfield, and his faith that God will protect us.

EULOGY

◆

The eulogy written by Count Valentine for his son. The paper is marked by tears. It lay unread in the fields of Burryfield.

Thank you to all who have attended today.

My son Johnathan was a great man, and a better son. These are simple words, but truthful all the same. He was a great man. He was a priest who cared for others more than himself. His joy in life was sharing the word of God, and seeing people accept the savior into their hearts. He was also a great son. I was not an easy father. My son made the best of it though, and taught me more than I ever taught him. His love and compassion got me through grave times. I wish he was only here now to help me with this.

Unfortunately, my son was taken too soon. Facing an unfair punishment from an unjust court. Even in his last days, he had faith in the Lord. Knowing that his salvation was guaranteed and that he had served him well. Even though I know my son would not want me to be distraught, I cannot indulge in that wish, for a father should never have to bury his son. I knew that this day would come, and I told myself I would prepare for it. It wasn't supposed to happen this soon. A shining light was dimmed too soon.

I have lived lifetimes. In those lifetimes, I have experienced tremendous loss and suffering. Incredible highs and splendid days. None of which compare to the experience I had raising you, and the grief I feel with your absence.

My son leaves behind a heartbroken father in his journey to a better place. I hope Helen treats you kindly and that neither of you worries about me. You both have helped me in my spiritual journey, and the battles I have with myself. If it wasn't for you two I would have continued to be lost.

I will continue the ministry I started for you. I am honored to follow in your footsteps. I will try to send as many good people as possible to accompany you. Thank you, Lord, for not punishing my son for the sins of his father like the members of this town. I will be back to visit you and your mother often.

ANGER

━━━━━◆━━━━━

A resignation letter from Father Grisham.

To Mr. Hornsworth,

I am leaving this note with you tonight to alert you of my resignation. After the events I saw yesterday, I think it might be best for me to distance myself from this ministry. Father Valentine was a kind friend of mine and a great priest. To think that the Church would go to such lows to destroy our cause. I cannot take such a risk.

I have left the money you have paid me in your bags. I have not spent any of it yet, and I assure you that it is all there. I'm deeply sorry for the inconvenience this has brought you in this dark time.

I know Count Valentine has left for the woods once again and wishes not to be disturbed. It is for this reason I have left in the middle of the night. I do not wish to see what evil returns from the woods. I had never seen such eyes of evil glow, until I saw his reaction to the noose prematurely releasing today. Not a drop of remorse in his soul, just pure anger and hatred. I do not wish to be in his path when he returns. I fear the ministry will see much more controversy following these misfortunes.

I hope my explanation proves my reasoning well enough. Although I will not be here physically, I will still be praying for all of you during these times. I believe you truly do want to spread the word and nurture it. The Church does not agree with your customs, though, and I will not jeopardize my life for your cause in good faith. It makes no difference to me if people hear the good word through the Church or your ministry. I am safer now with the Church and the authority it has over this country.

In my time with the ministry, I have experienced wonderful testaments of faith and trials that have grown a greater bond with my savior. I am thankful for these opportunities you and the Count have given me. Hopefully, one day we will meet again under better circumstances.

Father Grisham

Temptation

A conversation overheard at a tavern in Burryfield.

"Can I have one more please?"

"Thank you."

"I thought priests weren't supposed to drink?"

"We all sin on occasion."

"Alas, the bottle can tempt any man."

"Amen."

"Can I ask you something, Father?"

"I'm not on the clock."

"I don't want a sermon Father. Just a conversation."

"I'll tell you what. If you pay my debts here, I'll absolve you of all your sins, and answer any question to your heart's desire?"

"*Seems like a great deal.*"

"You do not know how deep my debt is."

"*Still, it can only go so high, and for pure redemption. To be absolved of all my crimes. I'm sure it is still a fine deal.*"

"So, what questions do you have for me?"

"*Just one, actually. How many souls have you saved?*"

"I don't understand your question."

"*How hard could it be? How many souls have you saved?*"

"I haven't saved any souls."

"*You made it to the rank of priest and haven't saved any souls?*"

"I do not save souls. Because, our savior is only capable of that. I'm nothing but a man."

"*Maybe it's my wording. How many men have you led to the savior? How many are you personally responsible for?*"

"I couldn't say. I don't see it like that."

"*Don't overthink it, Father. How many souls have you personally been responsible for saving?*"

"Zero. I have not saved a soul. I just try to preach the good word. The savior takes care of the rest."

"*That's incorrect, Father.*"

"Agree to disagree."

"No, Father. You see, each man is responsible for his own salvation. So you must have at least saved one. That being yourself. You are also a priest, though. So how many seeds did you put in people's hearts? So that the savior can harvest them? Father, I will ask you again. How many souls have you saved?"

"Well, I couldn't know for sure. Using your logic, I would approximate about twenty. Ones that I planted a seed in. Most people I preach to have already accepted the faith."

"And come to you for repentance and a weekly sermon so they can feel like they have completed their divine duty. I thank you for your honesty. Now ask me that question."

"Are you a priest?"

"No. I still have a tongue, though. I can still make words and make conversation with my fellow man. So ask me the question?"

"How many souls have you saved?"

"Three."

"Can I ask how you did it?"

"I was a priest for a short time. A long time ago. Few wanted to hear my message, though. They would rather beat me to a pulp than accept Jesus as their savior. Now I would like for you to ask me another question. How many men have I deprived of salvation?"

"What kind of game is this?"

"Entertain me for a bit longer. I'll pay for your tab the rest of the night."

"How many?"

"No. I want you to say it out loud. The whole thing. I want to hear you say it."

"How many men have you deprived of salvation?"

"Thousands."

"Is this some sick game to you? Do you go around and try to spook people for laughs?"

"Well I do find it humorous, but that is not my intent. Life is nothing but a game. A game that if we lose we are damned and one that if we win, oh then we are given eternal life."

"How much have you had to drink tonight?"

"I'm as sober as a priest. Oh, I guess I shouldn't use that as an example. Sober as a decent priest, I guess, would be the right comparison."

"I am a decent priest."

"Then why are you drinking, Father?"

"A friend of mine died today."

"Oh, that Valentine fellow?"

"He was a good man. I relied on him a lot for help through dark times. "

"Oh yes, the fire starter. Great man to help you through dark times. He'll simply light a fire, and then you'll be able to see again."

"He didn't start that fire. He couldn't have. He was persecuted since he was a threat to the Church. They would have pinned any crime that happened that week on him."

'I'm sorry, Father, but you are wrong again."

"I'm not wrong. I knew Father Valentine well."

"You don't think he could have been tempted with anything to start that fire?"

"What do you mean?"

"I convinced him to start the flame. He is not the man you think he was."

"That's not true".

"Sure it is. To be honest it was easier than I thought it would be. He had so much hate inside. He wanted to do it. To get back at them. He just needed a little shove."

"You're lying!"

"Am I? If so, you would have walked out by now, or possibly even have taken a swing at me for disparaging your friend on the day of his death. Instead, you stay and listen. Because in your heart, you know it's true. Or maybe you are so deprived; you'll allow any disparaging of your "friends" for a few free drops of ale."

"I don't even know who you are. How am I supposed to trust a word you say? Who are you? That could convince anyone to do anything."

"Leopold."

"You know of me. I'm sure that Jeremiah boy has whispered about his evening on the train. Or your old mentor, Father Abraham, I'm sure he told you about that farmer in the woods."

"Don't be frightened, Father. "God's" on your side. Now you know I'm serious. You see, Father Grisham, I was there. I take pride in it. You know how much fun it is to corrupt the soul of a holy man. I love it in a way that cannot be manufactured. It is only the product of true love for the craft. You can tell that, can't you?"

"So is that why you're here? To corrupt my soul?"

"No. Heavens no. I'm here to drink in honor of Johnathan Valentine. Another successful victim. Another soul that will be out of the grasp of God. Besides Father, I couldn't corrupt you any further than you have corrupted yourself."

"I'm not corrupted."

"Spoken like a true sinner. Lies come off your tongue easier than the sun rises each morning. Well, I must attend to other business.

The world has too much hope in it, a flaw I wish to exploit. Drink up, Father. Your tab will be paid for as I promised. Just make sure to keep your hands to yourself this time."

"Sir, could I please get another one?"

GREGORY FIELDS

The following announcement was hung throughout Burryfield. Many were trashed or burned in protest. Written by Benjamin Hornsworth.

To All Burryfield Citizens,

My name is Count Valentine. I would like to personally invite you to service this Sunday in Gregory Fields south of town. Service will begin at dawn and will continue until the tenth bell. The sermon will be given by Father Reynolds. A bright young priest whose enthusiasm for the Lord is sure to inspire you. Baptisms will also be offered at this time, utilizing the river that runs through the fields.

I know you have heard a lot of things about me and my ministry. I hope that this Sunday, I will be able to disprove a lot of these rumors. We are friendly people, and you have no reason to fear attending. All will be taken care of, and my ministry team will take the time to talk with anyone who wishes to engage with us after the service.

Do not bring money for tithing we do not accept it and will refuse any such offerings. If you wish to donate money to help the cause, please donate it to the cathedral's reconstruction.

Most of you are familiar with my son's passing and the public trial that preceded it. I have no ill will towards Burryfield or the Church. I still mourn my son and believe that he is innocent. He was taken too early, and I will forever miss him. He is in heaven now, and there is no better fate for such a man. These events will have no impact on the service, or the sermon given.

I hope that those who come will take this as a chance to praise God and lead those closer to the Lord. Although we do encourage believers to come, we do want to lend a hand to those who have never accepted the Lord into their hearts.

This is a chance for you to explore the wonders of faith without persecution. We are all sinners and do not wish to break you down. We will not shame you or let you leave feeling worse than when you first came. We just want to share the good word that has helped us. The word that allows us all to be saved and feel better. We don't want you to leave with guilt, but with hope.

Let all who are brave enough to attend be blessed and protected by the almighty himself.

Count Valentine

FATHER REYNOLDS SERMON

The following words were spoken to a crowd on a Sunday morning.

Good morning ladies and gentlemen.

On behalf of the Count Valentine Revival Ministry, I would like to thank all of you for coming here today. The city of Burryfield has been very clear on its position to our ministry. You all have taken a risk to be here with us today, and I thank you for this. I pray for your safety as you return home and that your dread doesn't distract you too much from my sermon.

We do not wish for you to come all this way, take the risks you have and get nothing in return. We hope that you will leave with salvation today, but I am a humble man and know my arguments here today may not convince you. We have brought loaves of bread and butter for a feast following the sermon. We will also be giving out the sacrament to those who wish to receive it. I believe that is all of the announcements I have to make at this time.

To start us off, I would like to read from Ephesians, chapter three, verses sixteen through nineteen. This is taken from a prayer that Paul writes to the Ephesians. I wish this same prayer for you.

That he would grant you, according to the riches of his glory. To be strengthened with might by his Spirit in the inner man. That Christ may dwell in your hearts by faith; that ye, being rooted and grounded in love, may be able to comprehend with all saints what is the breadth, and length, and depth, and height; and to know the love of Christ. Which passeth knowledge, that ye might be filled with all the fullness of God.

Today I want to speak to you of a great evil. An evil that enjoys diverting us from salvation. An evil that faces every man and woman. A powerful evil that many of us can be helpless to. An evil I wish to help relieve you of today. This evil goes by many names. It goes by shame, doubt, and the one I choose to focus on today, guilt.

How many of us have toiled with this evil when we try to get rest at night? It keeps digging at us, a constant gnaw on our consciousness. It's one of the worst enemies on our path to salvation. It's one of the worst enemies to even those who don't believe. I wish to share with you today the way to deal with guilt. Your best tool in defeating this sin.

Faith is the water to the fire that is guilt. Jesus Christ is your ally, not your enemy. Faith in him and his teachings are the only way to destroy this guilt.

We are all sinners, and we are ashamed of these actions. We seek forgiveness for our past deeds. In a time before the messiah, men would sacrifice animals for their sins. In Hebrews, it states that without the shedding of blood there is no forgiveness. Forgiveness is not a simple, easy act; it's a serious commitment. Now I am not telling you that you need to go home and sacrifice any worldly animal or child. I'm trying to convey that asking for forgiveness should not be taken lightly. It's still today as it was back then, a serious commitment.

Another passage. *For God so loved the world, that he gave his only begotten Son. That whosoever believeth in him should not perish, but have everlasting life.* John chapter three verse sixteen.

God is a kind father to all of us. No longer do we have to sacrifice our cattle for forgiveness. Because through God's forgiveness, he sent his only son. Jesus Christ, to die for our sins.

Christ shed his blood for all man so that we can have forgiveness. Every cross you see is a reminder of the sacrifice of Jesus Christ and that forgiveness is now attainable by all mankind. Faith in Christ is the only true way to have forgiveness. The only true way to defeat guilt is through this faith.

Recently I had a conversation with a man. A wealthy man who made his gains through illegal practices. A man who murdered for the sport of it. A man who used to spite God and committed a sacrilegious act every day. This man told me that he didn't believe that he could be saved. This man lost faith in God many years ago, so he feared that God had lost his faith in him. He told me that he knew that if he prayed, he would be forgiven, but that he doesn't believe he deserves forgiveness for his deeds.

Now the Bible mentions forgiveness quite a bit. It is an act we are supposed to show our fellow man. In it, you will not find one passage that speaks to forgiving yourself. The closest thing we have to mention of it is in the phrase, love thy neighbor as thyself. This means we must treat ourselves with respect and that we must be able to forgive ourselves. Surely we are expected to do this for our neighbor.

I would like to take the remaining amount of time of my sermon to talk about Peter, the apostle, how his story can explain how we can forgive ourselves.

Peter promised Jesus that he would never abandon him. That he will stay with him until death. Jesus tells Peter that this is not true, and that he would betray him when pressure was applied. When temple guards came to arrest Jesus in the garden. Peter was questioned three separate times if he knew Jesus. Peter denied ever knowing his Lord. That guilt ate Peter alive. He had turned his back on God's only son. Peter is not seen again in the good word until after the crucifixion of Jesus.

When Jesus returns later to the apostles, he questions Peter three times. The same question over and over again. Peter, do you love me? Peter confirms his love for the Lord, and his devotion. They say bad things come in threes, but they also say good things come in three. Peter denied the Lord three times, and Jesus questioned him three times. Important to remember the connection between these two events.

Jesus does not abandon Peter after his denial. He forgives him. The grace of God will always be enough for man. Let the overwhelming love of Jesus cleanse you here today. Jesus only asked one thing in return; to follow him.

Can man truly forgive himself? I'm not certain he can. I'm also not certain that it is his duty. God can forgive us if we repent, and ask for forgiveness. It is our faith in the Lord that allows us to be forgiven. If you truly have faith in the Lord, then you are to be forgiven. Your doubts and fears otherwise do not come from God but from an ancient evil, for God promises that he remembers your sin no more after you repent it. If you are truly a man of great faith, then your sin is forgiven.

Worries, guilt and doubt will always continue to plague us. It's human nature to worry. It is up to us what we do with them. If guilt was a spark that set your house aflame, would you let it stay and continue to grow into a large fire? Or would you simply put it out? At some point, the fire will seem too large to put out, but the love and grace of God is like an ocean. Able to put out any fire.

Let us pray.

Father who art in heaven, blessed be thy name. We come to you today, humble people.

We are all flawed and search for your guidance. We reflect on our past transgressions and ask for forgiveness. We pray that all your children will know for a certainty that they are forgiven. Give us all a strong faith. Amen.

Before I leave you here today, I would like to cry out to the crowd and ask if anyone here today is called to be baptized. If you have never accepted Jesus into your heart, it would be my honor to take this step with you today if you feel that you have strayed too far from the Lord and want to show your devotion in asking for forgiveness. I would also like for you to step up.

THE REVEAL

An entry in Benjamin Hornsworth journal.
The paper is now framed in the office
of the Bishop of Sundry.

Praise be to God!

The most remarkable thing happened today. An event I would not believe unless I was there to bear witness. Today in front of a crowd of people, in broad daylight, Count Valentine revealed himself to the public.

After spending the past few days in the forest alone, I feared I had lost him. That he might have abandoned the ministry altogether. I had never seen him as distressed as that day. A father who had lost his son. The only family he ever had. It was well within his right to be mad at the Church and the city of Burryfield.

But today, for the first time in centuries, if the stories I have been told are true. Count Valentine appeared in the daylight. Among men and women. It was astounding to see him there.

Father Reynolds called out to the crowd asking for people who wanted to be baptized. After silence for what felt like an eternity. A single man called back to him, asking to be washed clean of his sin. The voice I recognized. The voice of the man I had worked for the past thirty years, Count Valentine. He walked into the river with Father Reynolds. Prayed to the Lord for forgiveness for each of his own sins. Promising to accept his love and kindness. After which, Father Reynolds laid him in the water.

The smile on my master's face. I had never seen it before. It was one of pure glee and joy. He looked lighter, and the paleness of his face seemed to fill with color. It was a joyous occasion for all involved. The energy was infectious, and more from the crowd soon asked to be baptized. Those who had never accepted the Lord and Church members both went into the water.

Out of all who came, more than half were baptized. Even with the threat of violence when they returned to the city. It is the largest accomplishment of our ministry. Finally, we saw the fruit of all our relentless hard work and faith.

Lord, thank you for answering these prayers and letting your kindness shine through. I must remember this gift through the darkest days life has in store for me.

THE DANCE

———————◆———————

A poem from my personal collection.

Smiles begin,
With the tapping of feet,
For another sinner free of sin,
A dance of awe on the golden street.
Let us rejoice for our fellow soul,
Who once again has found his way.
In their new image they are made whole.
Who could not celebrate this joyous day?
Let us dance the sacred ballet,
In honor of the gift so prized,
We must entertain and display,
For a child of God has been baptized.

TELEGRAMS

◆

EMERGENCY SITUATION. FIRE IN SUNDRY. PLEASE SEND HELP.

-

PLEASE SPREAD WORD. FIREFIGHTERS NEEDED. WHOLE CITY A BLAZE.

-

MASS EVACUATION. CITIZENS MOVING YOUR WAY. MANY INJURED.

-

MASS CASUALTIES. NORTH SIDE OF TOWN COMPLETELY LOST TO FIRE.

-

LAST MESSAGE BEFORE EXITING. SEND EVERYONE YOU HAVE. LET GOD HAVE MERCY ON HIS PEOPLE.

WRATH

———————◆———————

A story, where friends reunite. One last time.

Leaves of the fall trees blew through the town of Burryfield. A reminder that the season of heat was coming to an end, and that it was time for the harvest. Nothing good ever happens after dusk on a Friday night. Most of the people of Burryfield had retired to bed. Only the drunks and night watches stayed up this late.

Count Valentine and his ministry were still not allowed in the city. They were forced to camp on the outskirts of town. The accounts of their sermon last Sunday did very little in the eyes of the Church or the city they controlled. The entire ministry was asleep besides Count Valentine. He had wandered off to the unmarked grave in the forest. It was his first time returning since his baptism.

"Helen. I'm sure you already know. You always knew more than me. Now hopefully, you look down with a smile. You don't have to worry anymore about me. I have faith again. Not just a belief, but concrete faith. I know God is real; I know his forgiveness is real. How much of a fool I have been to not partake in the love of the Lord. I wasted so much time. Now is no time to worry, though. It is time for me to serve; to preach during the day again. To once again spread his word, not through my money, but through myself. I know I will never get to see you again. I want your memory of me to be of a kind man. A man of great faith. I will miss you. Until next time my love."

Count Valentine stepped back from the tree that now rests over her body. It was simply a seed when he planted it so long ago. The tree stood tall, and firm. Its leaves had not yet left like the trees surrounding it.

The air was still. The night was cold, and Count Valentine looked out at the stars. They had changed since he was born. Another wonder of God, he thought to himself.

As he began to walk away, he heard the most devastating sound in the world. The laugh of an old friend. A chuckle of a low malicious tone. From behind that special tree, Leopold stepped out. His dark suit became a silhouette in the moonlight. A cigarette shined an orange light on his face. The smoke emanated from his face with pride. Valentine was sure that Leopold would appear sooner or later to try his evil tricks.

"You really think you changed?" Leopold snickered. The question was sent out with a shock-wave. Count Valentine felt true terror again for the first time in centuries. "To think God would ever forgive a sinner like you. You haven't changed from the man you once were."

"Leopold? I want none of your trouble. You should know better that I won't fall for your little traps. I taught you most of them." Count Valentine was brave in his speech. Even if inside, he felt his stomach tightening.

"Valentine? My sweet buddy ol' pal?" Leopold cried with glee. "We both know that I'm not talented to trick you. You have always been your worst enemy. You must not worry about me. For you would not fall for well-crafted stories. You wouldn't have a single doubt in your soul if I told you that your son was responsible for that fire. You would see right through that, wouldn't you? I have no reason to lie."

"Why are you here then? What game do you wish to play?" Valentine questioned the devil in disguise.

"Valentine, I have come to test your new salvation, and devotion to God. For I know there is still that beast inside of you, just wishing to be let out. Waiting for that one little shove. So much anger inside you. So much shame." Leopold's laughter rang through the trees.

"There is no need for such a test. I have left all of that in the past. I must leave you now." Count Valentine turned around and tried to make a quick exit.

"Wait Valentine." Count Valentine stopped in his tracks, knowing that this haunting was not done. "Don't you want to know why your son snapped so soon?"

"I figure you must be involved in some way." Valentine stayed with his back to Leopold. Not wishing to give into his game.

"A simple bribe to the executioner is all. He gave me a great deal too. Like most men in that town, he wanted to kill your son. Just needed some financial compensation for any penalties that came his way for the act." Leopold finished his sentence with a harshness that can only be described as a metaphorical hard bite.

The silence that comes with pain flooded the forest. Count Valentine took a deep breath before speaking. "My son is in a better place. He would not want me to get angry. In his honor I respect that. Goodnight, Leopold."

Leopold smiled. Although it turned out his work would be harder than he thought, he knew it would bring more satisfaction. A true challenge for him. The first in a very long time. "You still are an angry man with no plan of truly forgiving yourself. There is still guilt inside of you. Tempting you, telling you there's no chance for salvation. Might as well attack me. I'll prove that to you."

"There is no reason for you to cause pain to any innocent person. For nothing you do to me today or tomorrow and on will ever shake my faith. No longer will you haunt me. I'm born again. No matter how bad my pain, or any loss you bring my way. I will still continue to serve the Lord. Knowing that I am forgiven." Count Valentine spoke with confidence. For the first time in their interaction, he was in charge of the conversation.

"Let's see about that." With the flick of his wrist, Leopold sent his cigarette towards Helen's tree. A single spark ignited the oil he had laid down before. The flame ran up the tree, spelling the word "slut" with its path. The word makes Valentine's head drop. As the flames reached out to the branches, Leopold challenged his project again. "Which is more painful, Valentine? When you saw your son snap and flop like a fish? Or was it when your wife died of the sickness? I think my handy work was best with your son though. Watching the cathedral burn was so much fun. Made me want to do it all over again, but with your wife. Is this enough to get you boiling hot?"

Tears ran down the Count's face. After working up the will, he spoke. "All good things must come to an end. Nothing on this earth is ours to keep forever. Just holding it for the time we have. Leopold, I wish you well; I pray that you will someday see the truth. That God is not your…"

"The truth? The truth is that no matter what good you do in this world, you will still be punished. That this is all just some fucking game we play for his amusement. That joy is a fleeting emotion that was never meant to last?"

"Leopold. God is not your enemy. He is a loving God. You have always been so prideful. Never wanting help. You see that as a weakness. I saw myself as unworthy. God will forgive you if you ask?" Count Valentine extended his hand out to Leopold. The fire from the tree started to spread through the forest.

"Fuck you Valentine." Leopold withdrew a dagger from his pocket, stabbing Valentine in his hand. "You think a loving God would save me? A man who once crunched a newborn between his fingers just to hear the sound it made? Where was his love for that child? Or the parents? Face it Valentine; God abandoned us a long time ago. Mankind is far too wretched for his love or forgiveness. Instead of sending a flood, he sent those like Thomas George, Vlad the Impaler and Queen Mary the first. Those like you and me." Leopold starts to twist the knife around in Valentine's hand.

"You are wrong. He hasn't abandoned us!" Count Valentine pushes against the knife so hard that the handle starts to pop through the other side. His hand now rested on that of Leopold. "There is still a way for you, my brother."

"I wish it were true. We're both destined for an eternal life without God. We've both been cautious with our lives because of that. Making sure to live on as long as we can. What reason now do you have to keep running, Valentine? The way I see it, if you are serious about your commitment, I should just kill you right here and now. That way, you can see how God has abandoned you as you rot in Hell with your boy and that slut."

Count Valentine looked around the forest. The fire had grown into a mighty ocean of embers. The wind pushed the fire towards the city.

"I need to stay to serve. To help these people. We need to help them!"

Leopold laughed with a whimper. No longer as confident as he once was. "Count Valentine, man will help himself. We are cruel animals; the strong among them will survive. Let it play out the way God allows it. You can do nothing to save them. You will sit here with me and watch and see what your faith will do for them."

Leopold beat the legs of the Count with a burning branch before tying Valentine to a smoldering stump. Sat beside him and looked out over the city. Preparing for the reactions of the citizens below. Both men were certain they knew what would happen. One fueled by faith, and the other by doubt.

God Allows It

The following is an excerpt from the unpublished autobiography of Benjamin Hornsworth.

Of all my time spent with Valentine's ministry, there is one day that will always stick with me. It is a pillar of my strong faith today. We were located in Burryfield the night of the Great Fire that destroyed that once great city. At the time, it was a headquarters for the Church. The city of Burryfield today has tried to rebuild itself. I hope it once again reaches the status it once had.

To this day, no one knows what started the fire that night. I can attest that it came from the forest surrounding the mountains. As our camp was near the burning forest, and we were some of the first to notice it.

Some say that the fire was an act of hatred by the Count Valentine's ministry. Others said it was a lightning bolt sent by God to punish the city for its sins. The most probable case is, of course, that it was simply a forest fire. They are common in that area of the world. A careless camper or smoker.

When I first spotted the fire that night. I woke up Father Reynolds and Deacon Christianson. We ran down to the city to alert people and try to help with suppression efforts. The fire had already started to spread to some of the houses on the edge of town.

Church bells started to ring to wake up those still sleeping. Fear was spreading quicker than the fire. Screams of women and children could be heard all around us.

The firemen that the city had, as well as many other volunteers, fought the fire as best they could. In the end, the flame was too strong for them, and they had to eventually prioritize evacuation over preservation.

Deacon Christianson left with some firemen to help elderly residents get to the nearby river for safety.

Once the city was about a quarter demolished is when the chaos hit. Neighbors began betraying each other. Fathers fighting one another for goods. Thieves took the opportunity to rob houses. I even noticed one man stab another in the back repeatedly. Looking like he was doing it for the pure joy of it.

Father Reynolds and I were helping a small group trying to get through the violent crowd out to the river. Father Reynolds was holding a small child in his arms when we heard gunshots ringing out from the road laying ahead. We quickly decided to head down a side street to try to remain clear from the violence. Unfortunately, the fire got there first. The flames jumped over us while we were running.

Looking up, we realized that we were trapped. The flames on both sides of us caused everyone's vision to blur. In our straying from the crowd, we had run right into our demise. The children started to cough, and the mothers began to shriek from the fear. Some of the men with us decided to try to find a way out, but all ended up perishing.

That was supposed to be our fate as well. To suffocate from the smoke as our bodies withered away from the intense heat. We could only stand on the stone street since it wouldn't catch fire. It was still hot to the touch, though. The burning of fabric and flesh still lingers in my nose today. I can no longer have a fireplace or sit around a campfire. The smell brings me back to that fear.

We were all huddled in a circle. There were exactly twenty of us left in that street. Eight adults, twelve children. One of the mothers with us cried out to Father Reynolds. "Why would God let this happen?"

Father Reynolds' face showed pain and confusion. He too, was pondering the question. "I do not know," he replied. The child in his arms tightened his grasp upon him.

"Please, help me!" The little child said. It caught Father Reynolds by surprise. He felt helpless for a second before setting the child down.

"Everyone come together, hold hands. For when two or three are gathered in his name, there God will be with them. We must rely on God to save us." All of us in attendance could see the confidence in Father Reynolds' statement. It was infectious, and soon everyone felt sure that we would survive.

Father Reynolds began praying for the health of the children and to ease our fears. He prayed for one hour straight. For the safety of the town and to send angels to protect us. For those in the crowds to make it out alive and for those who perished to join his kingdom.

As he prayed, the most stunning miracle I have ever witnessed took place. The buildings on each side of the street began to die out. The ground began to cool, and soon we could each feel droplets of rain.

With the exits no longer blocked, we all successfully escaped out to the river. Families were reuniting with each other. The hope ran through the water of the river. Giving everyone their relief. The rain grew stronger, and we all sat silently along the riverbank as we watched what was left of the city of Burryfield slowly die out.

That was the last mission of the Valentine Ministry. That day was the last I had seen Count Valentine. I always was of the belief that he died in the fire, helping those who betrayed him earlier. He was, after all, a man of great kindness. Father Reynolds would later rejoin the Church and be sent away to America. Being one of the key players in the Church's expansion out in the West. Deacon Christianson would go on to leave the Church and found a small church in his hometown. A church he promises to welcome anyone. I still get correspondence from him occasionally. As of the time of writing this, he is doing quite well for himself.

That day was an end to an era. Allowing me to venture out into new possibilities. Some years later, I found out that Count Valentine had listed me as the inheritor of his estate and a small fortune. I used his gift to me to continue the work he started. Constructing orphanages and shelters for those in need; all bearing the Valentine name.

It is to Count Valentine, his ministry and all those involved that I owe my success and strong faith today. I thank God every day for bringing them into my life and sharing their loving influence with me.

The Burryfield Fire

An article from the Heethburg Gazette.

Last night after sunset, a forest fire struck the city of Burryfield, causing immense damage to the city. The City of Heethburg is asking for help in aiding the residents of the city.

"Many distressed people will be coming our way. Our neighboring city has suffered many unfortunate events this past few months. It is our neighborly duty to help aid them," Heethburg mayor Fredrick Smith, stated in a briefing to city officials last night.

The Church will be opening its parish doors to the citizens of Burryfield. Providing them with food and shelter for the winter. Donations are welcome to help in this endeavor.

"There is nothing left there besides a few structures. The fire swallowed the city whole.

It will take forever to rebuild, for right now. There is nothing there for us." Robert Howell, a lifelong citizen of Burryfield who escaped the city last night, commented to the gazette.

The fire has officially been suppressed by firemen of both Heethburg and Burryfield, as well as a rainstorm that came in the early morning.

As of right now, there is no official account of how many perished or were injured in the event. Several families are still trying to find their loved ones after the tragedy.

"Today will forever be associated with the great fire of Burryfield. It is a dark day for our country and for the citizens of the great city. I have faith, though, that this will not be the end. The city was born from a rebirth, and we shall do it again. It is our relentless spirit which makes us who we are," Mayor Wallace commented to a crowd in Heethburg this morning.

"We received an emergency telegram in the middle of the night from Burryfield stating there was a serious fire. I was in the bell tower when I got the news. I looked towards the mountains near Burryfield and could see the tips of flames peeking up from the other side. They must have been hundreds of meters into the sky. I'd never seen anything like it before," Cornell Lithiscs, a lamplighter, reported.

Firemen are camped out in the area to try and preserve remaining structures and help the wounded. Search efforts are already underway in the city, and notices will be put out in the surrounding papers.

FAITHLESSNESS

◆

The final terms of a deal.

"I told you. Look at all the trouble they cause. Murdering each other for what?" Leopold chuckled. He listened to the screams from the city with reverence. Dancing a small gig while taunting the Count.

"Have faith, Leopold."

"For what reason should I have it? God is allowing them to burn. Look at the fighting down there. Does it look like they have faith? That father abandoned his child, abandoned his boy. Just to not be singed by a little fire. What faith should I have in man after that?" Leopold looked out over the city as the clocktower fell on a crowd of people. The titian hue shined on his face. Revealing the face of a scared young man and the smile of pride. "Count Valentine, I tell you now that you are not saved. Look at what God has in store for the innocent. The ones who couldn't dare dream of the atrocities we have reveled in. This is the religious capital of the east? Look at what he has planned for his believers. Explain to me the reaction of these people. Are these the actions of a faithful people?"

Count Valentine sat against the stump, his flesh burning to the tree. He was unphased by the pain or the rants of Leopold. Sitting there, he smiled and had eyes of hope. "Faith isn't instinctual, it's something we have to work on. I have faith that it will turn around, I'm sure you can too if you wanted."

Leopold scoffed and replied. "What happened to you? You once were the evilest man I knew. A man I once feared. I have to believe your faith is fraudulent. That the monster inside you still exists. That you know you won't follow your commitment. That you will once again bring trouble into this world. What do you need me to do to prove that to you?"

"Leopold, no such argument exists that will cause me to abandon my faith again. I did not take this step lightly." Count Valentine began to laugh. "You want control over me, you want control over them. Everyone. Then you won't feel so weak. It's not your doubt that drives you. It's your fear of God that does." Valentine looked Leopold dead in the eyes. "You do believe he is still around."

"Foolish Valentine. That might have been true several hundred years ago. No longer, though. God has abandoned all of mankind a long time ago. Now I am in control. Look down at that city. Do you know how many of them are praying to God for help? When's the last time you saw him send angels down to help man? When was the last prophet he spoke to directly? It's plain as day that he has left us to our own devices. In this new world, I am a king. That is what I wish for you to see."

Count Valentine and Leopold sat atop the hill for another hour. Watching over the city as it burnt. No word spoken; only the occasional chuckle of Leopold broke the crackle of the flames and the cries for help. Valentine stood fast. He continued to silently pray to his Lord. For the survival of the people of Burryfield. While Leopold smoked a fresh cigarette and enjoyed the show.

The first raindrop that fell that night landed on Count Valentine's hand. He watched as it ran down his hand into the hole left by Leopold's knife. The second drop hit Father Reynolds, praying to a small group inside the city. The third fat raindrop hit the cigarette of Leopold. Extinguishing the light holding the heat inside.

The mountain soon was hit by a downpour of rain. It had been centuries since a rainstorm of that magnitude had hit the country.

"Leopold, therefore, I still have faith. God is still watching over us." Valentine grabbed the shoulder of Leopold. "These blessings could still be yours."

"Valentine, you still believe this is God? This is pure happenstance. It proves nothing. It won't be enough to stop the town from burning." Leopold's sweat ran down his face. His eyes trembled with fear.

"Call it what you will, Leopold. Whatever helps you sleep at night, as for me, I will call it a bountiful harvest of faith. You see, guilt will never go away; it just won't. But if faith remains, guilt will never be able to conquer." Valentine cries out to the heavens. "Thank you, God! Thank you for all that you do! Let your children bring praise to your name!"

Those were the last words of Count Valentine. The knife entered his neck, before being slashed down to his collarbone. Leopold spent that night destroying the corpse. He cut it up into several pieces. He smashed the heart under his boot. Threw his fingers to the inferno below. All the while, Leopold was still faced with defeat by the smile of Count Valentine. A man he had known for almost two thousand years. The smile of relief on his face sent chills down his spine.

A New Saint

SAINT GREGORY 1886
PATRON SAINT OF SACRIFICE

Saint Gregory was born in Burryfield and joined the Church at the young age of 15. He became a Deacon before his 18th birthday and a priest before his 23rd.

Saint Gregory spent his entire life and career with the Church in the city of Burryfield. Where he was known as an upstanding figure, who served the city as much as the Church. His selfless service is his strongest characteristic. It is noted this is what made the council decide to make him Bishop of the surrounding area.

Saint Gregory was most well known for being the Bishop during the Great Fire of Burryfield.

Witnesses attest to seeing him praying for rain near the remains of the Cathedral. Others claim that he offered himself up to God in return for rain for the others.

His body was never found. Many believe that his sacrifice is what caused the rainstorm that put an end to the Great Fire. Saint Gregory was officially canonized in 1942 by the Church for his courageous act of bravery and selfless service.

FRAUD

Baruch Dayan Ha-emet

Ahlan?

Who is it? Who's there?

Do not be afraid.

Where am I?

You are where you are meant to be?

Who are you?

Mavet

Do I know you?

You have not met me before. I have spent a
long time waiting for you.

You know who I am?

Orion Valentinos, son of Atlas Valentinos and
Sophia Valentinos.

I haven't heard that name in such a long time.

I'm sure you haven't. Language has lost its
beauty over time.

What is this place?

> You are now beyond the earth.

So, I am right in believing I'm dead.

> Do not fret. I come for you all.

So are you God?

> No, I wouldn't dare try and speak for Elohim
> hayyim.

Who are you then?

> Merely a guide to take you to your destination.

I don't understand.

> You will. Please follow me.

⌐

> I have followed your life with great interest.

**I know I must have sent many your way. I'm
ashamed of that.**

> That is true. You have lived more lives than
> many. There is a lot more to digest in your
> collection. It takes more time for cases like
> yours.

My son. Was he delivered to Heaven?

> I cannot reveal any information about the souls
> I deal with.

⌐

When will I arrive?

Not too much longer now.

Is it as bad as they say?

I do not know what it is you speak of.

Hell?

I cannot speak on it. I only transfer souls. I've never been into Heaven or Hell.

Can I ask you one last question?

We will be arriving at any point now.

What is God like?

Elohim hayyim is goodness in its purest form.

ㄱ

Well, you are here. You must take the following few steps alone.

This isn't what I expected.

The void is intimidating to look at, it is not as it seems.

This seals my fate, just going past this wall?

It is more a gateway to the other side.

So, this is it? This is the end.

There is no end to eternity.

ㄱ

I've missed you my sweet Valentine.

Epilogue

THE FAMILY CURSE

DEAR FATHER,

I know I haven't written to you often and that I don't often receive letters in response. However, I will continue in this endeavor. Since mother's passing, I have had no one besides my parish to talk to, and you are what is left of my family.

I write today not to belittle; I write to inform you of my travel. My new parish is still a work in progress. The Bishop of our town has sent me on a welfare check of an older member who lives atop a distant mountain. It's a two-day journey, and I will be staying in a hunting cabin the night thanks to a member of the Church. It will be the furthest away from civilization I have ever been, and I have been told that the paths can be rough this time of year.

I do not see this being a difficult trip, as you know though, pessimism is our family's curse.

So, I write to you in hopes of goodwill and to remind you that I am thankful for the lessons you have taught me as my father.

Peace be with you, your son Douglas O'Carroll.

THE MONSTER WITHIN

◆

The winter cold bit Father O'Carroll's ears as he walked up the mountain trail. Each step he took brought him farther from the city and closer to danger. He looked back at the city and was in awe. He had never seen Sundry from this high up before.

The sun was beginning to set as he watched. Father O'Carroll started to walk faster on his route. Not wanting to be stuck in the dark of unfamiliar territory. The sounds of the forest were enough to send him chills. He told himself it was nothing. He wasn't very convincing.

Snow started to fall when he was still a mile out from the cabin. His winter clothes began getting damp, leaving him with the shakes. His determination was that of a man trying to prove himself to his parish. Since his arrival, he had trouble fitting in with the other members, and a plethora of them started to visit other parishes. His dark complexion was still a troubling site to certain members.

The wooden door blew open when Father O'Carroll unlatched the lock. Snow started to rush in the dark place. Father O'Carroll lit a match near a nearby candle. As he tried to push the door against the wind, he could hear the howl of a wolf in the distance. It screams, giving him the extra strength he needs to accomplish his task.

The world went quiet inside the cabin. The whipping of the wind no longer permeated his ears. The candle on the center table was just bright enough to illuminate the center of the room without touching the walls. A black void lingered in their place.

With the aid of the candle, Father O'Carroll found the petite fireplace next to a small bed in a corner. His cold, fragile fingers barely managed to build the fire. He was exhausted after the voyage of the day. He dreaded the travel he had tomorrow as well. His eyes raced asleep.

A few hours later, Father O'Carroll heard the smack of the door opening once again. His eyes remained closed as he was still working up the energy to get up to close the door. The winds howling started to irritate the priest, but before he could get up to fix it the door closed on its own.

Father O'Carroll clenched his eyes in fear. Pretending that he was still asleep, that the events unfolding were just a dream. It's possible. The man had been haunted by nightmares since birth. The harsh sounds of snowy footsteps echoed in the cabin. Walking to the opposite corner.

Father O'Carroll tried to squint and see the intruder. The corner remained in pure blackness. He thought he might have seen the shoulder of a figure, but he was sure that his eyes were playing tricks on him.

"Help me!"

It rang into that cabin like a church bell. The pain of the voice shattered the soul of Father O'Carroll. It was the sound of his deceased mother. He knew that voice better than any other. "Mother. Is that you?"

There was no response, only silence.

Father O'Carroll got out of bed and made his way to the far back corner with the candle in hand. The silence remained. After several slow footsteps, he had reached the back corner. Touching it with his own hand. He was relieved it was just a dream.

When he turned around and had taken a few steps, he heard a sharp snap. It came from behind him. From the same corner, he had just touched. He was frozen in place. The bed and fireplace across the cabin seemed miles away.

He started to rationalize the experience. Thinking it must have been a tree branch outside breaking inside from the wind. It was just a coincidence. That's when he felt it. The subtle touch of something leaning on his back. When he turned around, he saw the dangling corpse of his mother. It was an image he had seen before. A year ago, when he found her in his family's cellar. The expression was still the same.

When he awoke the next morning, he was reassured that it was just a dream that his imagination was playing tricks on him.

Before leaving the cabin, he prayed on its porch. "Dear thou Father who art in heaven. I come to you in humbleness. I will admit, Lord that all I hear is silence. I'm never certain if a message is your divine intervention or just occasional chances manifested by nature. Last night I had a dream that has haunted me, it makes me worried about my journey ahead. I pray Father for good tidings, safe travel and for mercy. I pray, Lord, that I am able to engage in a good conversation with Mister Abraham and help bring us both closer to you. In your name, Amen."

Father O'Carroll was well on his journey when he approached the cliffs of the estate. Two hundred feet up in the air rested the small manor of Mister Abraham. "Hello!"

There was no response, only silence.

There was still a long trail ahead of the priest before he would reach the estate on top. As Father O'Carroll began to walk, he could hear the wind whipping in patterns. He didn't think much of it. Mister Abraham fell abruptly from the sky and hit the trail in front of Father O'Carroll. Abraham landed so close that the blood pooling touched the shoes of O'Carroll.

The cathedral doors in Sundry opened on the Friday following the incident. Father O'Carroll walked up the center aisle before resting on his knee to pray to his God.

There is no response, only silence.

Bishop Reynolds is greeted by three knocks on his office door. "Come on in." The door opened to show the face of Father O'Carroll. Sorrow still painting his face. "Father O'Carroll? I wasn't expecting to see you so soon. Please have a seat. How are you feeling?" Bishop Reynolds was accustomed to the Father's pain. He took a second before speaking. "A tragedy that you have seen can make many feel lost. I urge you to take your time to digest this hurdle. It's a hefty task, Father. I don't wish for you to feel burdened by the Church. No one is expecting a speedy recovery."

"I just don't understand, Bishop."

"What is it, Douglas?" Bishop Reynolds moved closer to the grieving priest.

"Why would a believer of the Church commit such an act? Does he not know that he sacrificed his salvation?"

"Well, he made his decision and knew the ramifications. He was a priest at one point and would teach it just as you or I." Bishop Reynolds sat thinking. "I cannot and will not speak on his why. It is not our place to understand."

"Mr. Abraham used to be a priest?"

"He was. A better one than I. Father Abraham and I would write correspondences with each other when we were both younger men. I always believed that if he hadn't left the ministry that he would have been sitting in this office, and that I would be coming to him for advice."

Father O'Carroll was so puzzled by his new information. "What made him leave the church?"

Bishop Reynolds sighed. "A while back he experienced a tragedy, not much different from the ones you have faced. After that he walked away. It was too heartbreaking for him."

"Do you know what that tragedy was?"

Bishop Reynolds' heart dropped. "I do." His eyes lingered to a dark memory. "I must not trouble you with any more bad news. You will become accustomed to it."

"You are the one who says, Bishop, that you would rather have your pipes leak on a rainy day than on a sunny one."

Bishop Reynolds chuckled in a light tone. "I can't argue against a man so wise. If you insist." The Bishop returned to his desk. Taking out a small bottle of cheap liquor he had kept for safekeeping. He poured a bottle for him and the priest. "Father Abraham was on a mission effort in a small village back in the old country. To put it plainly, it was not going well. He kept telling me that he couldn't get the seed of Christianity to plant there." The Bishop finished his glass and repoured himself a new one. "Until one day, he successfully baptized a whole family. When he returned later in the evening to break bread, he found the whole family burning in a fire on the property. Their bodies were mutilated. He was never the same after witnessing that. I was sent to replace him, and when I returned home, I was told he had retired."

Father O'Carroll's gloom and confusion only grew after hearing the story. "Do they know why the family was attacked?"

"No one knew. The townsfolk I talked to told me that Father Abraham had gone mad. That there was no such family. Abraham would later tell me that it was the patriarch who killed them.

That he saw the devil whisper in the man's ear. It's a shame, really. He could have helped save so many more if he had stayed with the ministry." Bishop Reynolds looked out his window, grieving the man he once knew.

Father O'Carroll ran his finger around his glass. "How could a man once so devoted lose his faith? It still puzzles me."

Bishop Reynolds returned his gaze back to the hurting priest sitting across from him. "Well, it's something I have pondered through my life." The smell of fire returns to the Bishop's nose. "Faith relies on the beholder. The man who has it. Man is tricky; man is also flawed. Inherently, sin will always corrupt every individual. Doubt will always sink in and has a way of toying with us. In the grand scheme of things, I believe that when faced with doubt, men usually fall into one of three categories. The first is impatient. The one who, to put it simply, cannot wait for faith. This person does not want to wait. Anger or fear takes control, and they decide they must take action to get what they want. Whether it's the justice they seek or an item they desire. They have no patience for God and his mysterious ways. They want it now, and so they abandon their faith. The second is the pessimist; those who can't see the brighter side. Those men do not have much faith as it is. The doubt doesn't cause them to act. It haunts them. It creates a stagnant man. It lingers and makes them ponder if there is a God. And if there is a God, will God save them? They wonder if God has abandoned humanity. Some men find it easier not to have faith. Because they don't want the chance of being wrong again, therefore, they leave it behind." The bishop finishes his second drink. He thought to himself if he wanted another.

"What is the third type of man?" Father Reynolds sat impatiently; wanting to know more.

"The last type of man is the relentless man. Every man will have to struggle with doubt. It's a monster inside us all. One that if we do not constantly battle, grows. We slowly become slaves to it. Its power over us makes it harder to battle. Doubt can make men do reckless things. Survivors though, they don't quit. They are relentless in the war against doubt. They might not win every battle. But they do not accept defeat. It's the war that matters most after all. They won't let their doubt intimidate them. If one can keep the spirit to fight doubt, well, then they keep their faith and persevere."

Father O'Carroll sat across the table, soaking in the words of the Bishop. "Which man do you think Father Abraham was?"

"Hard to say. Although I don't think it matters which he was. That is a question for the individual. I know which one I am. No one can truly know which one you choose to be except you and God. At times, even the individual might not know which they are." Bishop Reynolds saw in his eyes that the question was not truly about Father Abraham. The Bishop returns the liquor to his desk cupboard and finishes off the priest's drink. "You have had a tough couple of months, Douglas. You still have time left on your sabbatical. I will extend it if necessary. It's okay to be lost from time to time."

Father O'Carroll walked back down the center aisle towards the doors leading to the city. As he reached for the handle, he heard a poor woman crying in a pew. He made out a few words from her prayer.

"Help me."

The young priest turned around and went to comfort her. She cried on his shoulder until she felt the love she had lost.

There was no response, only silence.

VINCENT WEBSTER BLACK was born and currently resides in Western Montana, near Helena. He was raised in a "cult-like" environment and adopted at the age of 17. Vincent's work tends to lean toward the themes of guilt, shame, dread, and wrath. He is the creator of creepy videos online and short fiction published on his website.

www.vincentblack.net
Instagram: @vincentwebsterblack
Youtube: Vincent Black

Acknowledgements

It has always been a dream of mine to write a book. Although I have enjoyed writing short stories my entire life, I didn't think my writing translated well to a longer format. I guess time will only tell if I was correct. I would like to thank all of those who encouraged me to continue chasing my dreams, especially my talented fiancé Juliet whose love is more powerful than she knows.

9 798987 002605